The Left-Handed Dinner Party and Other Stories

The University of Alberta Press

The Left-Handed Dinner Party

and Other Stories

MYRL COULTER

Published by

The University of Alberta Press
Ring House 2
Edmonton, Alberta, Canada T6 G 2E1
www.uap.ualberta.ca

Copyright © 2017 Myrl Coulter

LIBRARY AND ARCHIVES CANADA
CATALOGUING IN PUBLICATION

Coulter, Myrl
[Short stories. Selections]
    The left-handed dinner party and
other stories / Myrl Coulter.

(Robert Kroetsch series)
Issued in print and electronic formats.
ISBN 978–1–77212–328–9 (softcover).—
ISBN 978–1–77212–346–3 (EPUB).—
ISBN 978–1–77212–347–0 (Kindle).—
ISBN 978–1–77212–348–7 (PDF)

    I. Title. II. Series: Robert Kroetsch
series

PS8605.O8935A6 2017   C813'.6
C2017–903274–7
C2017–903275–5

First edition, first printing, 2017.
First printed and bound in Canada by
Houghton Boston Printers, Saskatoon,
Saskatchewan.
Copyediting by Helen Moffett.
Proofreading by Meaghan Craven.

A volume in the Robert Kroetsch Series.

The University of Alberta Press is
committed to protecting our natural
environment. As part of our efforts,
this book is printed on Enviro Paper: it
contains 100% post-consumer recycled
fibres and is acid- and chlorine-free.

The University of Alberta Press
gratefully acknowledges the support
received for its publishing program
from the Government of Canada, the
Canada Council for the Arts, and the
Government of Alberta through the
Alberta Media Fund.

for Dad

Contents

Grad School

ON THE AFTERNOON of her twenty-fifth birthday, Patsy watched the family pass around her brand-new university degree. Uncle Hal read the inscription out loud. "Bachelor of Arts. Nice."

"And it only took six years," said Patsy's dad, with a wink.

"Why major in English? What's that good for?" said Denny.

"And what did you major in, buster?" said Patsy's mom.

As usual, Denny didn't seem to hear his mother's voice. "And a minor in Sociology? Are you some kind of shrink now?"

Their mom punched Denny's shoulder. "I wish. Maybe she could fix you."

The family stood on the grass outside Convocation Hall, surrounded by hundreds of other smiling families. Uncle Hal pulled out his camera. After snapping a few shots, he handed it to Patsy.

The four photos were almost identical. Patsy's parents looked stiff, like fenceposts. At one end, her father stared into the distance; at the other, her mother squinted into the sun. Only Denny grinned at the camera, holding two fingers above his sister's head in a crooked peace sign. The shortest member of her family, Patsy was dwarfed by her lanky parents and gangly brother. She handed the camera back to Uncle Hal.

"My eyes are closed in every shot."

Denny leaned in to have a look. "Yeah, and Shortcake needs a box to stand on."

Hal rearranged the group and took more photos. After that, they all went to a local bar and settled at a table on the rooftop patio to celebrate. The late afternoon evolved into one of those glowing June evenings when the air stays warm and the sun lingers long in the sky. After a pitcher of beer, they switched to margaritas, followed by a carafe of the house red wine. They staved off complete drunkenness by munching on three orders of nachos with extra beef and cheese.

"The first university graduate in the family. We're so proud of you, kiddo," Patsy's dad said, again and again.

Hal and Denny engaged in several rounds of arm-wrestling, nearly knocking over the almost-empty margarita jug and the carafe of wine. Their server came over and asked them to stop horsing around. That's when Patsy's mom ended the celebration.

"I have some news."

"Did I tell you how proud we are of you?" said Patsy's dad.

"Yes, Dad. Several times. You can stop now. Spit it out, Mom. What's your news?"

"I'm moving."

Patsy noticed her father's hands grip hard onto his chair arms.

"Moving? Where to?" she asked, looking from her father's end of the table back to where her mother sat.

"Prince Edward Island. Moving back home."

"I thought this was home. You and Dad are moving to PEI?"

"No. I'm moving to PEI. By myself. I don't know where your father's going."

Patsy looked from one parent to the other. Uncle Hal looked at the floor. Denny reached for the wine.

"I bought a boat," said Patsy's dad. "It's in Seattle. I'll live wherever it takes me."

"What about the house?" said Patsy. Her voice sounded small and far away.

"The neighbours bought it. Seems they've always liked it," said Patsy's mom. "Gave us a good price. Too good, I guess, if it bought your father a boat."

"You must have seen it coming, kiddo," said her dad. "Look on the bright side. You've got that shiny new degree, and a whole month to find a job and an apartment."

Patsy hadn't seen it coming. She was pissed at herself. How could she have missed the obvious?

| Getting an apartment was easy. Finding a job was not. Patsy sent out resumés to computer companies, insurance companies, and government departments. She didn't get one interview. Obviously, her brand-new university degree had done nothing for her job prospects. Why had she bothered? For the next year, she survived on part-time work in a coffee shop.

Her family had never been one that spent a lot of time together. Yet she felt alone, off-balance, unmoored. Her parents had vaporized, become disembodied voices and occasional pieces of mail. Patsy's mom phoned from Prince Edward Island at one o'clock on the last Sunday afternoon of every month. Her dad sailed his boat up and down the Pacific coast. Patsy received four postcards from him that year, one per season. In January, Denny went to Mexico for a vacation and never came back. He called his sister a few times. In a slurry voice, he said she should join him down there. She dreamed about her brother after each call, the same dream: she went to Mexico, found Denny's head on a deserted beach, but couldn't find his body.

Only Uncle Hal remained real. On special occasions, like Thanksgiving and Christmas, he took Patsy out for dinner.

"I'd call you more often, Shortcake, but I don't want to interfere with your love life," he said over a pub meal on St. Patrick's Day.

She didn't tell him about Troy, the Australian tile layer, who was arrested for identity theft while they were at the movies one sunny Saturday afternoon. Or Trevor, the bounty hunter from Idaho, who left in the middle of the night, taking her Visa card with him. After those two, Patsy promised herself no more men with "Tr" names.

At Easter, while they were out for pizza, Uncle Hal said he had a friend who managed the Greyhound bus office. They were looking for ticket agents, and the friend had agreed to interview Patsy.

| Three and a half years later, she was still at Greyhound, issuing tickets for places like Drumheller or Lethbridge or Kamloops or Dauphin, Manitoba. Occasionally people bought tickets all the way to Toronto or Montreal. She always looked at them for signs of desperation. Did they know how long they would be sitting on a bus? Patsy tried to calculate how long a bus trip to Prince Edward Island would take, but the route got so complicated that she gave up.

Her workday started at eight in the morning. Most of the time, she was punctual. But sometimes her alarm didn't go off, or she couldn't find her left shoe, or the line at Tim Hortons was longer than usual. She was late the morning the office got a new manager. When she walked in, he looked at his watch.

"Hi. I'm Travis and you're late."

"Sorry. Traffic was horrible this morning. There was an accident on the bridge. I'm Patsy."

He took her small hand in his. His lips released into a slow smile. "Accidents happen."

Travis was tall and long-limbed. He reminded Patsy of a long-distance runner, although she never saw him break into a jog, much less a full run. A few weeks later, he offered to buy her a drink after work. Soon Friday nights became their regular time—until he told her that he couldn't see her anymore. He didn't think it would be right while his wife was pregnant.

Patsy was late for work on Monday. Everything went wrong that morning—there was another accident on the bridge, and the whole world was in line at Tim Hortons. When she finally got to work, Travis reprimanded her in front of everyone.

"Expect accidents. Leave home earlier, and do without your coffee. You can make up the time over lunch today."

Before she could stop herself, Patsy let loose in her loudest voice. "Is it necessary for you to be such an asshole?"

That afternoon, the bus company fired her for insubordination.

| Months of job-hunting followed—months of submitting resumés, and getting no callbacks and no interviews. Patsy became convinced that the only way people got jobs these days was by knowing someone, or having an uncle with connections.

Patsy needed money, so she put her stereo up for sale on Kijiji. A job ad caught her eye: *Don't want to be fenced in? Like to drive? Call this number.*

The interview took place in a Starbucks, at a corner table. She wore a grey suit she borrowed from a friend, and high heels so she'd feel taller. He wore a Hugo Boss suit and Ray-Ban sunglasses. His name was Brandon, and he said he was a venture capitalist. His work required him to send and receive many packages, mostly documents, occasionally product samples, like exotic salts or organic grains. He needed a courier, someone with a clean driving record, someone he could trust.

The meeting lasted ten minutes. Brandon asked her how much she wanted. She shrugged and quoted the same amount she'd made at the bus company. He nodded. The hours were flexible. The job came with a smartphone and a leased BMW. How bad could it be?

A month later, Patsy didn't know anything more about Brandon's business than she did on the day of her interview. She hoped it was legitimate, told herself she was lucky to work for a reclusive rich guy. If she did her job well, he'd gain confidence in her, maybe promote her to vice-president or something.

Her instructions always came by text message, and her workday tasks seldom varied. She was given a map showing twenty-six locations, each one designated with a letter of the alphabet. They were all in industrial parks out past the suburbs. She never saw any people. She walked through unlocked doors into empty retail spaces, where bulky envelopes and heavy parcels wrapped in plain brown paper waited, tagged with post-it notes scrawled with her name. Twice a day, she made drop-offs at Brandon's house.

Soon Patsy suspected she was being followed. Sometimes it was a silver pickup truck, sometimes a black one. They both had tinted windows, so she couldn't see the drivers. She saw the silver one at one of her first location. Then she saw it again in traffic behind her. When she changed lanes, it did too. The next day, the same thing with a black truck, the day after that, back to the silver one again. She was pleased with herself for noticing the obvious. Brandon probably wanted to monitor her movements for a while. She'd show him she was reliable.

| On the morning of her thirtieth birthday, Patsy woke up with a sore jaw. She held her index fingers on the joints, gawed her mouth open and shut several times, feeling and hearing the clicks. *Maybe that's what happens when you turn thirty. On the exact anniversary minute of your birth, your jaw starts to click and irritates you for the rest of your life.* Then she saw them. Three coarse spirally grey hairs, sticking from the top of her head, waving for attention among all their brunette cohorts. She plucked them out and scrubbed hard at her scalp in the shower.

At Tim Hortons, Patsy counted the people in line ahead of her. Four. Out the window, she could see the drive-throughers waiting in their idling vehicles. Patsy suspected Tim Hortons spiked their coffee with a secret ingredient guaranteed to turn customers into addicted slaves, and always insisted on adding her own cream and sugar. She refused to be slotted into a category along with the other one sugars or two creamers, to be just another double-double puppet. Patsy unclenched her jaw again and took a test sip.

Her phone beeped with a message: "3 locations q x z"

With her phone in one hand and her coffee in the other, Patsy pushed the door open with her butt and emerged into the cloudless day. The sun already felt hot. Today would be another scorcher. Maybe the heat wave was getting to her. Maybe that was causing her jaw to ache, and her hair to sprout grey. Maybe turning thirty had nothing to do with it. She looked down at her sundress and felt good. A birthday present to herself, it showed a little cleavage, but not too much.

That's when she walked into the policeman's chest. A full-frontal body collision. For a brief moment, they both stood looking down at the brown stain across the front of her new white dress. He apologized several times, offered to pay for dry cleaning, to buy her a fresh cup of coffee. He had friendly eyes, but she shook her head and walked away.

"Anytime," he said, calling after her. "I'm here every day. Name's Jack. Again, I'm sorry."

Both her tailing vehicles showed up that morning. The black pickup truck was in the parking lot at her first location, the silver one at the next. Heading back into town after her last stop, Patsy saw the black one again in her rear-view mirror. She decided today was the day to talk to Brandon about it. Until then, he might as well know everything she did.

She pulled into a parking lot. The black truck did too. Inside the grocery store, she tossed a loaf of bread, two cans of ravioli, a bag of potato chips, and some dill pickle dip into a basket.

Standing in the express line, the one for fifteen items or less, Patsy counted fourteen items in the cart ahead. As soon as the cashier began to ring up her order, the woman ran off to grab "one more thing." The cashier bagged the woman's groceries while everyone else in line waited.

Patsy tapped her foot and looked out at the parking lot. The black pickup truck was still there, the silver one now right beside it. Finally the customer reappeared and put five more items on the counter.

The words came out of Patsy's mouth before she finished thinking them. " That makes nineteen items, not fifteen. And most people finish their shopping before they get into line."

Everyone turned to stare at Patsy. She shrugged and pointed to the express sign. "Read it. Fifteen items or less."

The woman held up her hand and gave Patsy the finger.

"Aw, come on," said Patsy. "It's my birthday."

" Then buy yourself a cake, honey, and quit hassling people."

Her phone beeped with a new message: "where r u?"

Patsy arrived at Brandon's house and got out of her car. The sun blazed high, obnoxious in a sky screaming for clouds. Up and down the street, each manicured yard was deserted, every front door closed. She wobbled a bit on her way up the sidewalk, juggling the weight of the three parcels. The front door of her boss's stone mansion was unlocked. Inside, she placed the packages on the granite bench in the foyer. She looked at them for a moment, trying to imagine the organic flour they contained. Then she punched a message into her phone: "pkgs delivered. can i talk to u?"

The return text came immediately: "wait outside"

Patsy walked back out to the street and leaned on her car. From a grassy park across the street came the sound of small engines. Patsy noticed two riding mowers crisscrossing the green expanse, driven by two young men. No—not men, boys. Probably high-school or college students lucky enough to snag outdoor summer jobs working for the city. Both were shirtless, wearing only work boots, blue jeans, and helmets. Their arms and shoulders were muscular. Athletes, Patsy thought. Or bodybuilders. Wide grins showed on their faces. They seemed unbothered by the heat of the day or the sweat pouring down their chests. She watched them toss small stones at each other. They reached into their pockets for hidden caches of ammunition with one hand as they manoeuvred their mowers with the other. The stones ricocheted off wheels, fenders, boots, arms, and helmets. Cranking hard on their steering wheels, they carved erratic zigzags around the park. Shaved grass fragments flew up in emerald eddies behind them.

Patsy drank in the scene as if it were lemonade. An old man on an old bicycle rode by, slowing to watch the action. When they ran out of stones, the two drivers dispersed to opposite ends of the park. At exactly the same moment, they took dead aim, gunned their motors, and raced toward each other, veering off only at the last second, huge grins still visible beneath their helmets. And then it was over. The duel was done, not won or lost, just finished. They shifted their machines into low gear, pulled up beside each other, and bumped fists.

Patsy studied the grass. The once overgrown park showed an uneven series of streaks, missed tufts of grass, and mounds of clippings ready for a mulch pile. By comparison, the orderly striations visible on the neighbourhood's well-tended lawns now looked plain, lacking zest, without verve.

She crossed the street, walked out onto the mown grass, and took off her shoes. Following the circle marks, Patsy broke into a slow run, then accelerated to a sprint as she replayed the scene, arms stretched out wide into the curves. The boys on the mowers applauded her performance.

That's when her tailing vehicles showed up. The silver pickup parked right in front of her BMW, the black one behind it. Her car was now sandwiched between the two trucks, with no room to manoeuvre out. Two men with shaved heads, both wearing muscle shirts and sunglasses, got out and disappeared into her boss's house without looking at her.

Seconds later, Patsy heard her phone beep with a new message: "come in now."

Her response consisted of two words. She pressed send, faced Brandon's house, and held up the BMW keys, dangling them in the air. Then she hurled them across the road into the park, and tossed the phone onto his lawn. Flanked by the boys, one mower on each side, Patsy walked down the deserted neighbourhood street.

After a quick stop at her apartment, Patsy waited for three hours at the Greek tavern where she was to meet Uncle Hal, sipping lemonade and feeling safe in midst of the beer-drinking crowd. When her uncle arrived, he ordered wine and her favourite Greek salad with meatballs. During dinner, Patsy showed him the birthday card she'd received in the mail. On the front was a picture of five dancing margarita jugs. Inside was a photo of Denny with his arms around two bikini-clad girls. Uncle Hal laughed when Patsy said she was glad her brother's head was still attached to his body. She didn't tell him that she wanted her head to remain in the same condition. Instead, she asked a favour. "Can I stay at your place tonight? I'm feeling a little lonely."

"Happy to have you, Shortcake. Anytime."

The next morning, Patsy took a bus from Uncle Hal's to Tim Hortons, where a policeman named Jack bought her a cup of coffee.

The Remedy

THE TRIANGLE OF BALLS broke so hard that three clattered to the floor. Doc glanced over at his only remaining customers: Guy, lanky and hard; and Ginger, a bottle redhead in tight satin pants. Guy demanded another drink.

"Bar's closed. Go home to your wife and kid."

Doc watched them stagger across the parking lot to Guy's sleek black muscle car, then locked the door and poured himself a Scotch. Grabbing a broom, he began his closing ritual—sweep and drink, drink and sweep. Murky visions of another wife and kid invaded his mind, along with images of him puking beside the front steps of the house he used to own, of his shaking hand ringing the doorbell. He could still hear the echoes of his twelve-year-old daughter's voice when she opened the door but barred his entrance: "Finish puking first, Dad."

Doc paused mid-sweep and looked around the empty pool hall. She'd be eighteen now, old enough to order a drink at his bar. Like him, she was left-handed. He hoped that was the only genetic trait she'd inherited from him. To quiet the chatter in his head, he focused on stacking chairs upside-down on tables. Then he continued sweeping and drinking. Several hours later, he too staggered across the empty parking lot, to an old grey Econoline van.

| Faint light glimmered in the eastern sky when the Econoline's door slid open. Doc rolled out and vomited on the pavement. When his stomach settled after its last heave, he reached behind a "No Parking" sign for his hidden hose and rinsed the pavement clean.

Doc was behind The Cue Ball's bar when Louise arrived for her shift. She put on her apron and eyed him as he unloaded the dishwasher.

"Did you go home last night, or just puke in the parking lot again?"

His response was to hand her a tray of clean glasses. As she reached up to slide a wineglass into the rack, the sleeve of her blouse fell back. Doc saw fresh bruises on her upper arm.

"You been in a fight, or did you just fall down the stairs again?"

Louise pulled her sleeve back down.

Doc unlocked the front door and the first customers of the day strolled in. One had red-rimmed eyes. He was sweaty pale as he leaned over the bar.

"Doc, I need your remedy bad."

Regulars at The Cue Ball knew they could rely on Doc. The concoction was his personal recipe. After years of tinkering with the mix, he'd perfected it: lemon-lime Powerade, tomato juice, Tabasco sauce, a can of sardines, and crushed aspirin, all pureed in a blender and garnished with a pickled asparagus spear. Doc passed the glass into shaking hands.

"Eat the asparagus. Helps with hydration. And go easy on the hard stuff today."

"How about one for yourself, Doc? You don't look so good."

Doc shook his head. "I work better this way. More efficient."

| That evening, Guy strode in at the end of Louise's shift. Doc watched him put an arm around his wife, saw Louise squirm away.

She put her hands on her hips and faced her husband. "Where've you been? Molly has been at home waiting for you."

Guy shrugged, moving in for another squeeze.

"Can't a man hug his wife without getting a lecture?"

Louise pushed him away. "You said you'd take Molly to a movie after school. She was counting on it."

"Nope. She'd rather be with her friends than me."

"She's twelve, Guy. You're the parent."

Another shrug. "My dad didn't bother me too much when I was a kid. I'm giving her the same benefit."

"Things have to change."

Guy glared at Louise and pointed his index finger between her eyes. "And my mom didn't bother my old man too much, either."

Louise glanced over at Doc, still watching them from behind the bar. "I have to go. Molly's been alone long enough. Come home and spend some time with us."

"Sure. Be there in an hour."

Two hours later, Guy was still playing pool. By then, Ginger had appeared, clad in leather pants, a tank top, and shiny boots with stiletto heels.

Two more hours passed. Ginger and Guy were again the only customers left, draped over each other on a pool table in the back corner. Doc decided to shut the place down early. Then he saw the minivan pull into the parking lot.

| Louise and Molly got out of the van and peered through The Cue Ball's window. Doc was wiping down the bar. In a back corner, illuminated by a pool table light, Guy and Ginger were only too visible. Molly kicked at the pavement in disgust.

"I hate him."

"You can't hate him. He's your father."

"He's a drunk and a sleaze and he hits you. Why do you stay with him?"

"We're a family."

"He doesn't want a family. He wants his laundry done."

Molly walked over to Guy's car, ran her hand under the fender for the hidden key box, unlocked the driver's door, and pulled an overnight bag from behind the seat. "See this bag? It's his stash. Clean underwear and smell-good stuff for his nights out screwing around."

Molly reached into the bag and pulled out a can of shaving cream.

Louise looked through pool hall window again. Guy was still oblivious to anything but Ginger's leather-covered ass. Turning back to Molly, she took the can from her daughter's hand and started shaking it.

"This car is his vintage pride and joy. Let's do it."

Louise sprayed shaving cream all over the car and used her finger to write "Pig" in the white foam. Then she and Molly deflated the car's rear tires. For the finishing touch, Louise dumped the contents of Guy's overnight bag onto the pavement, and spent the next five minutes stomping on his clothes, grinding them into the grease-stained asphalt.

| As soon as the minivan drove away, Doc announced closing time. The moment Guy and Ginger were outside, he turned off the lights and locked the door. Then he stood in the dark, watching Guy's reaction. Doc smiled as Guy kicked his flat tires and flailed around looking for a weapon. When nothing leapt into his hand, Guy yanked Ginger's purse off her shoulder, and swiped it across the shaving-creamed windshield. After Ginger had reclaimed her purse and stomped away, Doc turned his attentions to his closing ritual.

The next day, Louise arrived at work wearing too much makeup and a shirt with tight-fitting long sleeves. Doc threw her a questioning look. She held up her hand to silence him.

When Guy came through the front door that evening, Doc asked Louise to get some peanuts from the back storeroom.

"I'll get right on that," she said, not moving as Guy headed straight for the bar.

"Doc. A glass of your remedy. Right now."

Doc shook his head. "Not a chance."

"What the fuck?" said Guy, leaning over the counter.

"I don't serve cowards."

"Who are you calling a coward?"

"You. Get out of my bar."

Guy reached over and grabbed Doc by the neck of his shirt. "Make me."

Doc made no attempt to release himself. "I don't have to make you. They will."

Guy looked around. Doc's customers had formed a semi-circle, each brandishing a pool cue. Guy released his hold on Doc's shirt and held up his hands.

"Just kidding, fellas."

Nobody moved.

"Come on. Who's up for a game? Mike? Mac?"

They pushed in closer, moving Guy away from the bar and toward the door. Backed into a forced exit, Guy's face darkened as he flung out his parting words. "You're losers. All of you. Losers hanging out in a dump."

Doc poured a round of free drinks and sent Louise home early. Soon The Cue Ball settled back into its usual sounds of quiet chatter, punctuated by cues hitting balls, balls sinking into pockets, muted chuckles, and random beer belches.

At closing time, Doc let his remaining customers finish their games. After they'd gone, he drank and swept, swept and drank. A wave of nausea hit him as he crossed to the Econoline. A vehicle pulled into the parking lot and caught Doc in its head-lights. Louise and Molly emerged from the minivan in time to watch Doc vomit onto the pavement.

"We came to thank you," said Louise. "I—that is, we— kicked him out."

Doc straightened. "Good for you," he said, swallowing another heave.

"Why do you stay here night after night? Why don't you go home?"

"This is my home."

Louise opened the minivan's back door. "Get in. There's a room in our basement."

All was quiet. Doc shifted from foot to foot, looking at the ground. Louise kept her eyes on Doc.

"Adults are so stupid," Molly said.

Doc finally looked up. "Not a good idea, Louise. I'm too old to change. Too hard on the system."

Louise grinned at him. "You're not a coward, are you?"

He grinned back. Then he shrugged and moved toward the open door of the minivan.

Molly blocked his way. "Finish puking first."

The Left-Handed
Dinner Party

DINA SPINETTI DREAMED almost every night, macabre, murky visions filled with talking wolves and leering vampires that felt so real she was surprised they weren't standing in her room when she woke up. Now she lay sprawled across her bed, one eye half-open, trying to focus on her clock radio's limey-green numbers: five five eight. Two minutes before alarm time. Two minutes to listen to the magpies squawking from her neighbour's spruce tree. Two minutes to hover between worlds, between the shattered fragments of her dream world and the looming fragments of her real world. She didn't want either. What she wanted was more sleep.

Moments later, wrapped in her housecoat, Dina stood in the hall between the doors to her daughters' bedrooms. She rapped on each one at the same time.

"Rock and roll, you two," she called as she padded off to the kitchen.

As she stood at the sink looking out the window seeing nothing, Dog nudged Dina's leg. Six months ago, the girls had begged for a puppy. She'd agreed, but only after making them promise they would feed, walk, and clean up after it. They'd both nodded solemnly as they crossed their hearts and hoped to die.

Feeling Dog's tongue on her hand, Dina shuffled her feet into flip-flops. The early June morning was cool but held the hope of warmth to come. They walked to the end of the street and back. Dog dashed through the grassy front yards unleashed. When she pooped on the neighbour's lawn, Dina pulled a plastic bag from her pocket.

Back inside, Dog followed Dina into the kitchen. She put the turkey sandwiches she'd made last night into the girls' lunch bags, adding two juice boxes, plus an apple for Oldest and a banana for Youngest. After lining up the toaster, peanut butter, and bread on the kitchen counter, she padded back down the hall. Still no sounds coming from either of her daughters' bedrooms, so she opened both doors. Dog scooted onto Youngest's bed.

"Breakfast is ready, girls. Up and at 'em."

The clock in her room now glowed six-thirty. Dina showered and opened her closet door. She wanted to look good today. At work, it was decision day for a major contract, and tonight she was going to a potluck dinner party with her three best friends. She pulled out her grey business suit and put it on. Then she made her bed and laid out her new blue jeans and orange swing blouse, ready for a quick change tonight. She looked in the mirror. Hair up or down? Dina felt freer with it down, tumbling around her shoulders. But that was for tonight. For the office, she twisted the thick dark mass into an upknot and fastened it at the back of her head.

Back in the hall again, Dina sighed. Still no movement from either bedroom. She reached into the linen closet for the megaphone she'd used when she coached Oldest's soccer team, and raised it to her lips.

"Fire!"

Heavy thuds sounded as feet hit the floor in both rooms. Dina tried not to laugh as she brought the funnel to her mouth again. "Sorry. False alarm."

"Not fair, Mom!"

Two doors slammed in her face at the same time. She had to say goodbye through wood again. "I'm off, girls. I'd better not get a call asking why you two were late for school for the third time this week."

Her low-slung coupe prowled up the hill out of the neighbourhood. As always, while waiting at the first traffic light, Dina thought about the satisfying secret she took with her everywhere she went—a well-stocked trunk containing all she'd need if she were to disappear, even for only one day: a cotton T-shirt and comfortable jeans, running shoes and cozy socks. Last week, she'd added a fleecy jacket and a bucket hat. Two days ago, she'd thrown in a backpack, a water bottle, some granola bars, and Gloria Steinem's book about life on the road. These were her "just-in-case" items: just in case one day, on her way to work, at the intersection where the main road ran through the city, she didn't take the right turn that led to her office. She'd turn left instead and head out into the countryside. To where, she had no idea. She hadn't made it that far yet.

| Almost twenty years had passed since the day after her high-school graduation, when Dina dined with her parents and younger brother, as she had every other Sunday of her life. It was the only day they all ate together because Dina's father worked late at his office every night. Dina's mother called these weekly dinners family time, but Dina thought of them

as interrogation time. Her brother was only ten and fully
focused on food, so she was usually the target of their parents'
questions.

"Tell us everything, Dina. How was your big graduation
night?"

"The grad part was fine. But a boy in my class killed himself
at the bush party afterwards."

"That's terrible. Did you know him?" said Mother.

"Everyone knew him."

"Young people these days," said Father, shaking his head.
"A lost generation. Pass the potatoes."

"What a shame for his family," said Mother. "We're lucky
that you have a good head on your shoulders, dear. You'll need
it while we're away this year."

"Away?".

"Yes, your father has had a big promotion. We're moving
to London for a year. That's London, England, not London,
Ontario." Her mother's smile was so big, all her teeth showed.

"We've leased the house," said Father. "The boy will have to
come with us. You'll be fine at Grandmother's."

A week after her parents left, Dina paid two hundred dollars
for her grandmother's ten-year-old Pontiac. She crammed
everything she owned into it, waved at Grandmother, and was
soon heading west on the Trans-Canada Highway. The first
time she stopped for gas, she found an envelope in the glove
compartment. Inside were four crisp one-hundred-dollar bills
and a note in Grandmother's handwriting: "Keep it between
the lines, honey."

| Dina lingered in her look to the left until the car behind her honked. She turned right, and arrived at her desk on time.

The call came moments after she sat down. For the past three months, every day, and sometimes well into the evenings, Dina had worked on the furniture specifications for a renovation project at a prominent law firm. Last week, she had presented her quotation to the managing partner and his team. She knew her products were strong, and the pricing right where it should be. The presentation had gone well. She'd answered their questions without hesitation, and they'd all smiled at her as she left.

This morning, Dina made her voice light, ready to go into the usual banter where Managing Partner would ask how the battle was going, and she'd say she wasn't sure, but thought she was winning, and they'd both laugh. Today, his opening line was different.

"Bad news. We're going with your competitor's deal."

She felt her throat constrict. "Can you tell me why?"

"Don't take it personally. We were very impressed with your proposal."

"So why buy from the other guy?"

"I have no choice. This is a high-profile project. I play golf with him every Saturday. How could I face him if we gave it to someone else?"

"Then why did you come to me in the first place?"

"Business as usual. My partners expected a comparison bid."

Dina's stomach collided with her heart.

"Besides, the other guy has a family to support. He doesn't have two ex-husbands." His laugh roared into her ear. "That's a smart move on your part, Dina. If one support cheque doesn't come through, you've got the other one coming in. Everyone should have two ex-husbands!"

Within half an hour, Dina was summoned to the corner office, where Boss reacted badly to the lost contract.

"Maybe you'd better take up golf," he said. "Now get out of my office and go find some new business."

| On the drive home, Dina still felt sick about losing the deal and decided to skip the dinner party. She didn't feel up to talking tonight. When she walked into the house, Oldest and Youngest daughters were lying on the couch watching the first Harry Potter movie. They didn't take their eyes off the television as she kissed the tops of their heads.

"This one again? You must have the dialogue memorized by now."

The girls bore a striking resemblance to each other even though they had different fathers. Dina was secretly proud that they both looked like her, as if she'd produced her children all by herself. Their fathers continued to participate in their daughters' lives when they could, but they were both busy with careers and new wives. Dina was usually the only parent at soccer games and school meetings.

Being single didn't bother her. She'd always been more comfortable by herself. During those tedious "health" classes back in school, as various teachers talked their way around the touchy details of sexual activity, Dina began to think of herself as created outside of sex, self-born, materialized on this earth fully formed and capable. Perhaps she took that feeling into her marriages. She often told her friends that she took full responsibility for both divorces, how she shouldn't have been surprised that once married, her husbands expected her to turn into a wife and mother—and still be a lover. Her friends always laughed when Dina admitted that she could never figure out how to perform those roles to anyone's satisfaction, least of all her own.

She put the girls' pizza into the oven and reached into the refrigerator for some celery to smear with peanut butter. Celery was the only undisguised vegetable her daughters would eat. Her eyes fell on the salad she'd already made for the potluck dinner. Maybe she shouldn't cancel after all. The salad was ready, the girls were engrossed in Harry, and her friends would make her feel better.

She changed her clothes, put the pizza on the table, and called the girls to dinner.

"I'm going out. Clean up the kitchen. Walk Dog. And do some homework."

They moaned their responses.

"Call me if you need me."

She knew they wouldn't call, would leave their dirty dishes on the table. Homework would remain untouched, and Dog unwalked. She also knew they'd stay on the couch watching movies until they heard her car in the driveway, and dive into their beds just before she walked in.

| This dinner party was planned a week ago, while the friends were helping one of them move. Their packing instructions were to leave an adequate share of the household goods for an estranged husband they all detested. The friends obeyed those instructions, but with their own caveat: the clear glasses and undamaged dinnerware went into the moving boxes; the cloudy glasses and chipped plates, they left for him.

The wine was already flowing when she walked in. Hostess took Dina's salad bowl and handed her a glass of cabernet sauvignon. Dina took a long, satisfying swig and swirled it in her mouth before swallowing.

"Ah. Nectar," she said, looking around at her friends.

The strange ebb and flow of female friendship had often mystified Dina. In groups, she felt stymied, unable to find a graceful way into closed ongoing conversations. But these women were different, somehow. Dina was more than comfortable with them, all so unlike each other. Curvy Earth Mother, still married to her high-school sweetheart, was a mother of three who recently started an office job after ten years at home. Soft-spoken Hostess was a speech therapist who'd finally ended her marriage to a relentless womanizer. And Willowy Beauty was a personal trainer about to marry husband number four. Dina was unconvinced that number four was different from numbers one, two, and three, but she kept that to herself.

"Toast time!"

The four women raised their wineglasses in their left hands, their quirky group signature.

"What are we toasting?"

"Do you remember that first lunch we had, five years ago, the moment we all picked up our soupspoons?" said Earth Mother.

"Yes," said Hostess. "The waiter said a table full of left-handed women was an omen of bad luck and refused to serve us."

"I remember the very generous tip we left for the brave waitress who took us on," said Beauty.

"A toast to our powerful coven."

"To our coven." They clinked again.

"And remember our trip to the mountains last summer?" said Dina.

"Yes! I was so nervous about hiking because I was having my period, and I'd heard that the scent of menstrual blood attracted bears."

"How we howled when we found out we were all having our periods that weekend!"

"We figured no bear would be foolish enough to tangle with four cranky left-handed women. But we made a lot of noise as we walked."

"To bloody left-handed women!"

They refilled their glasses, sat down, and passed their potluck dishes around the table. Eating did not slow their conversation.

"You truly are amazing," said Beauty to Hostess. "Only here a week and already it smells like home."

"I sprayed the place with air freshener. I hate that stuff, but this place always smells musty. I haven't figured out where it's coming from yet."

Hostess raised her glass again. "A toast to my amazing friends. I couldn't have survived the last few years without you."

"Here's to survival," said Beauty, draining her glass.

"Amen to that," said Dina. "Let's look ahead, not back."

She turned to Earth Mother. "How are things at home now that you're working in the nasty corporate world?"

"Hank calls me every day to ask if I've quit yet. But yesterday afternoon the kids only called twice."

"What's Hank doing tonight?"

"He's at a cocktail party right now, a client-appreciation night. I'm supposed to be there, too."

"Those things are overrated."

Dina avoided the social networking scene. She hated cock-tail parties.

"How was your trip to Vancouver this week?" Dina asked Beauty.

"Heaven. We walked around Stanley Park holding hands. Shopped on Robson Street. Had room service in our hotel."

They all groaned and stabbed at her with their fork-wielding left hands.

" Tell us about your week, Dina," said Beauty. "How many dragons did you slay?"

"No dead dragons this week. Just more of the same. As soon as one battle is finished, another one pops up."

"If anyone can handle it, you can," said Earth Mother. "I wish I had your stamina."

"I agree," said Beauty. "Dina, you're the strongest person I know."

" That's what we love about you," said Hostess. " You don't need anybody."

Dina dropped her fork. She looked down, but couldn't see where it had landed because her eyes had filled with tears. Dina never cried, not even alone in her bathroom, much less in front of others. She rose from her chair, tripped over the table leg, and stumbled again as she grabbed for her purse. Rushing down the sidewalk, Dina heard Hostess's voice calling her name from the front door. She dropped her car keys and scrambled to find them in blurry darkness.

| The next morning, Dina backed her car onto the front street. She never went to a car wash. Doing it herself, with her own hands, was something she looked forward to. The first thing

every Saturday morning—spring, summer, and fall—while the girls were still asleep and the day fresh, Dina spent an hour with her car. She hosed it down, lathered it up with a special brush, rinsed it off, polished it with slow firm strokes, and buffed it with an old chamois left behind by one of her ex-husbands. She couldn't remember which.

Today, she scrubbed the chrome grill until her hands hurt. She'd been at it for about half an hour when she bent down to plunge her sponge into the bucket, and saw three pairs of feet. She looked up, and there stood her friends.

Together, they polished the wheel rims until their fingers were numb. Then they did the interior—the dashboard and steering wheel, the insides of the doors. They vacuumed the floor mats. And vacuumed them again. Finally, Dina opened the trunk and shared her satisfying secret. Beauty said she'd never need anything like that, but Earth Mother confessed to having one just like it.

Once they were finished, they all sat on Dina's front steps for an hour, talking while they drank coffee from a thermos Hostess had brought. After they left, Dina made two phone calls, one to Grandmother, the other to a realtor. That afternoon, a FOR SALE sign went up on her front lawn.

On the weekend of the "Mammoth Left-Handed Losers' Garage Sale," Dina sent Oldest and Youngest to spend time with their fathers. Garage sale aficionados lined up first thing in the morning. By late afternoon, they'd sold almost everything. Then they ordered in Thai food and turned up the music. Dina, Hostess, Beauty, Earth Mother, and Dog danced until the full moon was high in the sky.

| Two weeks before the end of the school year, Dina dressed in the grey business suit she'd worn the day she lost the big deal, and knocked on the door to the corner office. Boss accepted her resignation without looking up from his desk.

"No need for two weeks' notice. You're done today. Hand your keys in to administration."

That night, Dina cleaned out her closet and stuffed all her business clothes into a green garbage bag. Tomorrow she'd donate them to the local women's shelter.

The day after school was out, Dina backed out of her driveway, a small U-Haul trailer attached to her car. She paused a moment beside the SOLD sign, then drove up the hill. Oldest and Youngest sat sulking in the back. Dog rode shotgun in the passenger seat. At the intersection where the main road ran through the city, Dina looked right toward downtown. And then turned left.

The Scream

ONE WINTER, Beth Skinner noticed that her mother had become clumsy. She stumbled often. Scissors, baking pans, and potted plants slipped out of her hands. Marjory shrugged off her daughter's concerns.

"Oh, honey. So what if I tripped a few times? It's nothing. My biggest problem is that I can't sew in the basement any more. It's not warm enough. My hands get so cold, I can't thread my needle."

That's when Grant, Beth's father, decided to convert half the garage into a heated sewing room for his wife. And so "Big Roy" Biggs entered their lives. Grant hired him to do the garage reconstruction. An electrician by trade, Big Roy had massive shoulders and a deep hearty laugh. Beth heard that laugh most evenings. She would often come home from work to find Big Roy sitting in their kitchen, a cold bottle of Molson Canadian in his hand. Beth's mother invited him to stay for dinner one night. From then on, he was often at their table.

Big Roy prided himself on his ability to do electrical work without turning off the electricity. One day, he almost electro-cuted himself, and Grant started calling him Sparky: "Sparky jumped a foot in the air and cursed a blue streak you could hear two blocks over."

At dinner that night, Marjory said, "Big Roy, I like your work and your company very much, but cursing is not allowed in my house."

Big Roy didn't laugh at this. "Yes, ma'am," he said. Beth never heard him curse again.

Despite his cavalier approach to shocking himself, Roy was a conscientious worker. He paid attention to detail and took his time getting things right, so much time that more than three months passed before the sewing garage was finished.

Marjory was thrilled. She kept her new sewing room so warm that Beth, Grant, and Big Roy called it "The Sauna." But Marjory continued to stumble, and her hands were still cold. When she was diagnosed with multiple sclerosis, Beth and Grant learned everything they could about the condition. They wanted to be prepared for what lay ahead. Grant brought Big Roy back to widen the bathroom door and build a wheelchair ramp into the house, even though Marjory didn't need a wheelchair. "Yet," she said, ever pragmatic.

Beth commuted to her office downtown. It never occurred to her to move out of her parents' house. She couldn't imagine living away from them, felt no need to leave their tidy little bungalow. During the second renovation, Big Roy again lingered at the Skinner house in the evenings, chatting without cursing, as if he had no place else to be. When Beth came home, she often made dinner for four. She didn't mind. Cooking each night allowed her to shed the daily pressures of her job on the distress line at a suicide prevention centre.

"Why do you want to work there?" asked Big Roy. "That's gotta be tough."

"It is, but I don't mind."

"I admire you for that. Takes a special person to listen to panicked people."

"A boy Beth went to school with committed suicide," said Grant.

"Yes," nodded Marjorie. "It was a terrible thing. And on graduation night, too."

"He wasn't your boyfriend, I hope," said Big Roy.

Beth shook her head. "No, but I wish I could have helped him somehow. I see my job as an opportunity to do that for others."

| Marjory's condition stabilized. By the end of the year, she was doing so well that Grant took his wife on a week-long trip to the Rocky Mountains. A lifelong prairie girl, Marjory had always wanted to see the mountains in winter. They asked Beth to come with them, but she declined. Although she did want to visit the mountains, she thought her parents should enjoy a little time to themselves.

The Rockies put on a spectacular winter show for Grant and Marjory, dazzling white against the bluest of skies. They saw deer and bighorn sheep on the snowy slopes. It was everything Marjory hoped it would be. But on their way home, they got caught in a sudden prairie blizzard, and their car hit a patch of black ice.

The police knocked on Beth's door late that evening. When they finally left, the first person Beth called was Big Roy. He accompanied her to the morgue, and went with her to the lawyer's office to retrieve Grant and Marjory's wills. Five days later, he sat beside her at the double funeral.

For the next six months, Big Roy called Beth every week. On Friday evenings, they sat at the kitchen table and shared a beer. They often talked about electricity. Big Roy was a curious tradesman, a lifelong student of all things electrical, from eels to lightning. He explained alternating and direct current, conduction and circuits. The sound of his voice made Beth feel calmer, as if things were like they had always been. Sometimes they'd remember something Grant or Marjory said or did. When that happened, Big Roy's big hand slid across the table to cover Beth's, just as her father had often done when she'd had a stressful day on the suicide line.

But Big Roy took a contract job up north, and had to leave town. For several months, they kept in touch by phone once a week. Then once a week became once a month, and once a month became once in a while, and once in a while became never.

| Eight years after her parents' accident, Beth was promoted to manager of the suicide prevention centre. On a slate-grey winter day that brought only six hours of daylight, Beth was at her desk doing paperwork after a long shift on the phones. The distress line supervisor came in and sank into a chair in front of her desk.

"What's up?"

The supervisor sighed. Her eyes were moist. "It's bad, Beth."

"Who?"

"Your guy. Third time not so lucky."

The forty-five-year-old father of three had been one of Beth's success stories: she'd talked him out of two previous attempts. This time, he had hung himself using a belt his wife gave him for Christmas.

Beth's left eyelid began to twitch. It didn't stop until she got home an hour later. As she climbed into bed that night, her body started to shake, and her breath came in huge gulps. The episode lasted half an hour. The same thing happened every night that week. Each morning, her eyelid started twitching again.

The following Monday, Beth resigned and walked away from the only place she'd ever worked. One month later, she started a new job as the administrator in an assisted-living residence for seniors. She had the walls in her new office painted a soft yellow, a friendly colour that made entering the room feel like walking into a smile.

The previous administrator had a print of Edvard Munch's *The Scream* hanging in the office. Beth took it down and put in storage. This was a place for sunshine yellow and sky blue, not for screaming. On the wall behind her desk, she hung a print of Claude Monet's *Water Lilies*, the one with ivory blossoms floating on a blue-green background. Across the room, above a small round meeting table, she placed a print of Van Gogh's *Sunflowers*. She'd brought them both from home, where they'd long adorned the feature wall in Grant and Marjory's living room. When she looked at the blank spaces they left, Beth wondered if it was time for her to move. The thought always paralyzed her.

For her new job, Beth dressed in tailored navy-blue pant-suits, and fastened her mother's pearls around her neck. She was thirty-nine now, almost forty. Old enough to wear pearls, capable of the quiet dignity they represented. Or perhaps in need of it. After the chaos of the suicide centre, Beth wanted calm. She wanted her residents to feel that they lived in an oasis of serenity,

Beth settled easily into the flow of life in a seniors' complex. Three times a day, in the morning, at noon, and before she went home, Beth took a walking tour around the building, noting how much lighter her footfall felt here.

" This place has a cozy feel," she said to her assistant.

The assistant gave Beth a skeptical look. " This is a good day. We have bad days, too."

"I know. They're inevitable. But we're ready for those. Our goal is to create comfort every day we can. Our residents have earned these gentle years."

Beth kept the rest of her theory to herself. These were elderly people at the end of long lives, coasting to their earthly departures. Losing one of them had to be easier than losing a young person to suicide, or both parents in a car crash.

One wing of the residence was for the able, those who were still mobile and competent. They came and went as they pleased. Sometimes they popped into Beth's office to make requests. Would she mind asking the chef to make the soup less salty? Could she please arrange for a John Wayne movie weekend? One man arrived at her door distraught because he'd misplaced his copy of Pierre Berton's *The National Dream*. Beth spent half an hour helping him find it. He rewarded her with a lollipop he pulled out of his trouser pocket.

The other wing of the building was the secure unit. The residents here couldn't leave unless accompanied by a caregiver or family member. Every morning, after her tour through the independent wing, Beth entered her security code into the panel beside the door of the unit. Inside, she walked the wide hallways, dropping into each room as she went. Some occupants sat in front of television sets that went unwatched as their owner's chins rested on their chests. Some residents lay on their beds, a few asleep, others gazing at the ceiling. Beth made physical contact with each one, touching arms or hands as she said soft hellos. Many of their faces bore blank dazed expressions, and Beth realized that life's biggest loss was the thinking mind. When that went, the lived life went with it.

| Two months into her new job, Beth went to welcome a newcomer to the secure unit. A pale woman of about Beth's age twisted a pair of gloves in her hands as she stood next to a white-haired man slumped in a chair, his arms clasped across his chest. When he looked up, Beth recognized his eyes immediately.

"Big Roy!"

He looked up, but the blank look on his face didn't change. The woman introduced herself as Roy's daughter, Faye. Beth was surprised. She'd never heard Roy mention a family.

"I'm so pleased to meet you, Faye. Your father is a longtime family friend."

By now, Faye had almost twisted her gloves into a knot. Beth reassured her. " We'll make him as comfortable as possible here. Try not to worry."

"It's so expensive. We had to place Dad here privately because the waiting list for a funded spot is so long. Dad's savings are limited. My brother and I are pooling our resources to pay for this. It's a strain."

| From that day on, Beth concluded her morning tour of the secure unit with a visit to Roy. Emerging from her hallway stroll, she'd see him waiting for her in the dining area. It was

between mealtimes, so all the other tables were empty. Cutlery clatter leaked out from behind the kitchen door.

As she passed the coffee station, Beth poured two mugs. She felt Roy watching her every move. Once they'd both had a few sips of coffee, their conversations were brief and concise.

"How was your night, Roy?"

"Coffee's too hot."

"Did you sleep well?"

"Cold egg. And hard."

"I'm sorry to hear that. Did you eat it?"

"I'm not a son-of-a-bitch."

"I know that. You must have been at Shirley's table this morning. She doesn't know what she's saying, Roy."

"Lord love a duck."

Beth laughed, and thought she saw a fleeting smile cross his face.

"No cursing allowed," he said, his mouth cracking into a full grin as he met her eyes.

Beth was delighted to hear the echo of Marjory's edict, and clapped her hands: "You do remember!"

| Back in her office, reading through Roy's file, Beth pieced together the missing fragments of his story. His wife had died about ten years ago, before he came to work on Grant and Marjory's house. His son lived on the west coast, and had not visited since Roy moved in here. Faye resided in a small town a few hours south of the city and drove up to see her father once a week.

Before moving into the care unit, Roy had lived alone in a small apartment. As his dementia progressed, Faye had arranged for homecare workers to come in every day. But Roy always found a reason to send them away: they were too young, or they didn't show up on time, or their English wasn't good enough. Soon Faye gave up on homecare and paid Roy's neighbour a small stipend to check on him twice a day. But after a fire broke out in Roy's kitchen, everyone knew that he could no longer live alone.

At the back of Roy's file, Beth found a transcript of his cognitive assessment interview.

Thank you for coming in this morning, Mr. Biggs. This won't take long. I have just a few questions for you. Okay?
My neighbour is waiting for me. Fred.

Yes, I know. Before we start, I'm going to ask you to remember a sentence. At the end of our session, I'll ask you to repeat it to me. Do you understand?
Yes. Do you understand?
(Note: The interviewer laughed.)

No, that's not the sentence, Roy. Do you mind if I call you Roy?
Just don't call me late for supper.
(Note: The interviewer laughed again.)

Roy, the sentence I want you to remember is this: The bus stop is on the corner. Can you repeat that for me?
The. Bus. Stop. Is. On. The. Corner.

Excellent. Okay, let's start. Where do you live, Roy?
Out there (pointing to the window). Wind howled last night. Going to be a big flood year.

What do you have for breakfast each day?
One poached egg. Soft in the middle. And bacon. Crispy.

What do you do after breakfast?
I like chicken noodle soup too. For lunch. Settles my stomach.

Can you tell me what day it is?
My wife died on a Saturday. Nine and a half years ago. It was raining.

Can you have a look at these three animal drawings for me?
(Note: Mr. Biggs glanced briefly at the drawings.)

Can you point out the lion for me?
My son moved away. He has a new wife. I know what a lion looks like.
(Note: Mr. Biggs pointed to the camel.)

Okay. Let's move on. Here's a pencil and paper. Can you draw a clock for me?
It's ten o'clock.

I know, but I'd like you to draw a clock for me anyway.
(Note: Mr. Biggs drew a circle and wrote the number ten in the middle of it.)

Okay. Let's move on. Here's a telephone. Can you dial your phone number for me?
555-6396.

Good. You know your number. Now, can you dial it?
(Note: Mr. Biggs held the phone in his hand, but did not dial.)

*I'll take the phone now, Roy. Just two more things. Can you make
a scissor motion with your hand?*
(Note: Mr. Biggs did not react.)

Use your fingers, Roy.
(Note: Mr. Biggs touched the ends of his two index fingers
together.)

*We're almost finished. Just repeat the sentence I asked you to
remember at the beginning of our session.*
I have to go now.

| The following week, Beth noticed that Roy's hand shook more
than usual as he raised his mug to his lips. She also noticed that
his glasses were streaked with dust. So many of her residents
wandered around wearing smudged eyeglasses that Beth had
started carrying a small lens-cleaning cloth in her pocket.

"May I?" she said, leaning forward. Roy allowed her to
remove his glasses.

Beth rubbed the thick lenses and studied the man sitting
across from her. A few wiry eyebrow hairs escaped their thick
grey bushes, but his eyes were still the same brilliant blue
she remembered. Marjory used to say that Big Roy had Paul
Newman eyes.

Glasses back in place, Roy struggled to his feet. Beth stayed
in her chair, knowing he didn't want help. She watched him

make his way from the dining room to the hallway. His body was no longer straight and tall, his labourer's muscles long gone. The shoulders of his brown shirt hung halfway down his arms and his khaki pants were loose around his hips, held in place by a belt cinched at his waist. She wondered if he was counting his steps as he went. For many dementia patients, the numbers stayed as the words disappeared. Counting steps created a mind map Roy could use to find his way back to his room. Several times along the way, he reached out to steady himself on the wall. Beth made a mental note to get Roy a walker.

| When Roy didn't show up for coffee the next morning, Beth went to his room. It was empty. She knocked on his bathroom door. No response came, so she went in. Also empty. But the telephone that usually sat on Roy's nightstand was in the sink, and the sink was full of water. This was his second phone since he arrived. He'd washed the first one, too.

As Beth drained the sink, she looked down at the toilet. The framed photographs of Roy's family that usually sat on his dresser were in the bowl. That's when Beth realized that Roy hadn't tried to wash his phone. He'd drowned it, along with the pictures. She called maintenance and went to look for Roy.

Back in the hall, Beth saw a resident returning from a morning walk, accompanied by her daughter. They were an incongruous pair because Shirley was a big woman, and her daughter petite. Beth moved down the hall to open the door to Shirley's room. The daughter visited her mother every day, taking her outside for a short walk around the block.

"How are you today, Shirley?" asked Beth.

"Son-of-a-bitch! Go to hell! Goddammit!"

Whenever one of Shirley's swearing streaks began, her daughter would quietly plead with her mother to lower her voice. "Sssh, Mom," she said, before turning to Beth. "I'm so sorry."

"It's not your fault," Beth said. "Believe me, this is no one's fault. Have you seen Roy?"

A few minutes later, she found him at the exit door. He was standing in front of the security panel, punching random numbers into the keypad, trying to find the code that would set him free.

| Over the next few weeks, Roy became quieter. His contribution to their morning conversations decreased to a few short words and grunts. His new walker helped him get around for a while, but soon he became too unsteady to use it alone. After that, he accepted Beth's help.

One morning, Roy was completely silent. His jaw was clenched and his knuckles white as they gripped the walker's handle. Once he tried to pull away from her arm, but nearly fell over. When they reached his room, Beth helped him sit down on the edge of his bed. She sat next to him and put her arm around his shoulders.

"It's okay, Roy. Everything's going to be okay," she said. Her empty words hung in the air.

For the next half an hour, they sat in silence. When Roy's head rolled forward, she let him fall gently onto his side, pulled his legs up onto the bed, and covered him with a blanket.

A week later, Roy could no longer stand up by himself. His walker went unused. The staff brought him to the dining room in a wheelchair.

The following week, Roy no longer knew how to use a fork or spoon.

A few days after that, the staff had to stop feeding him by mouth because he'd forgotten how to swallow.

On the morning Big Roy was transferred to an auxiliary hospital, Beth watched the ambulance drive away. As it disappeared down the street, her hands flew up to her face, and she felt Edvard Munch's scream coming on. Her left eyelid began to twitch.

Uncanny

EMILY GOODWIN WAS NOT SURPRISED when her friendly UPS deliveryman arrived at her door in the middle of the afternoon. He said she should be working instead of shopping on eBay, and winked as he walked away. But the package he left in her hands wasn't from eBay. Emily recognized the deliberate handwriting, the unique wrapping style, the leftover yarn used as string.

Back in her den, she snipped the yarn and struggled through the patchwork of brown paper and old liquor store bags, reversed to hide the "Don't Drink and Drive" lettering. In the box she found a folded note atop a mound of tissue paper.

Emily dear, I thought you should have this. Mother.

Emily eased the vintage black top hat out of the box. In immaculate condition, the felt was smooth and smelled of mint. She lowered the hat onto her head. It settled easily into place, a perfect fit. As she studied her reflection in the mirror, a loud whistle, like that of a train, shrieked through her mind. She swiped the hat from her head. It flew across the floor and ended up teetering back and forth in the corner.

"Thanks a lot, Mom." She scooped the hat up, shoved it in the box, put the lid back on, and went back to work.

Emily's first-year English class was a tough slog this term. Twenty-seven essays sat on her desk, twelve in the marked pile, fifteen in the unmarked pile. With another batch due at the end of the week, she had to get through these in the next two days. Emily reached for the next one and began to read. The first paragraph didn't make sense. She read it again.

Margret Attwoode was a Canadain writer who wrote alot of books. Mrs. Attwoodie puts alot of insex and stuff in her imagry that she makes with words.

Insex? Insex? Oh. Insects. Emily groaned and read further.

Mrs. Attwoode likes insex just like that Shakespeere guy likes knives and ghosts that stings just like a green hornet high on bubbly suckt from the jug.

Incoherence from a university student. Why did it continue to astonish her?

| Sam dumped his hard hat on the floor and kicked off his boots. "Em?"

No answer.

He found her in the den and planted a sloppy kiss on her cheek. She didn't look up. He whispered in her ear: "Got a minute for the guy you live with?"

"Always, Sam," she said, without looking up from her work.

"What are you doing?"

This time, she did look up. "Watching soap operas. How was your day?"

"The usual. Over budget and behind schedule." He spied the box on the table and shook his head. "We talked about this, Em. You have to break your eBay habit."

"I didn't buy it. It's from my mother."

Sam rustled in the box and pulled out the hat. "Hey, this is pretty swank."

He put it on. She stood up and pulled it off him.

Sam laughed. "Okay...let's see it on you."

He tried to put it on her head, but Emily knocked the hat out of his hands. Sam jumped back. "Whoa...what's going on?"

She avoided his gaze and sat back down at the desk.

"Em...talk to me."

No response. Sam persisted. "Hello in there..."

"It was my grandfather's hat."

"I should have known." He retrieved it from the other side of the room. "You don't see many of these anymore."

"He had a whole closet full of hats. Always wore one."

"That figures. I felt like he expected everyone to call him Sir."

"I was lucky. I got to call him Grandfather Sir."

"Why would your mother send you his hat?"

"I don't know, Sam. Maybe she's cleaning out the attic again. Maybe she likes going to the post office."

"Or maybe she'd had her gin."

"You know my mother doesn't drink anymore."

"This isn't going to send you off the deep end again, is it?"

"I didn't go off the deep end. I was just sad for a while."

Sam picked up the hat and stood in the doorway with it tucked under his arm. "If this is going to make you 'sad' again, I'm getting rid of it right now."

"No. Leave it. I'll be fine."

Sam tossed the hat onto the table. Goddammit. That's all they needed—his whacko mother-in-law sending them Grandfather relics. The next mailed treasure might be dead

Dad's suicide note. Emily was distracted enough these days. He wanted to pick up the phone and tell the old lady off. But he wouldn't. Yet.

"Maybe you should sell that hat on eBay. There's probably some sucker out there who can't live without it."

| Emily spent all evening at her desk. Too many hours passed before she placed the last marked essay on the heap. Tomorrow she'd return them to her students. They wouldn't be happy. Her eyes fell on the hat as she turned out the light. What was her mother thinking? She climbed the stairs to join Sam, already asleep on his side of the bed.

Her body was weary, but she couldn't get comfortable under the covers. A breeze rippled the sheer curtains at the open window. She forced herself to lie still, take deep breaths, let the night air soothe her brain. Sleep came slowly.

Emily heard the faint sounds of drums in the distance. A gust billowed the curtains into the room. The sounds grew louder, and a glow lit the ceiling. In a crescendo of wind and rhythm, three red-coated drummers wearing pith helmets appeared and marched to the end of the bed. Emily's legs shifted under the covers. Her arms flailed. Her head turned from side to side, knocking the pillow to the floor. Sam slept on undisturbed.

Grandfather Sir was a tall gentleman with sparse grey hair and a well-trimmed mustache. Wire-framed spectacles perched on his nose. He wore a tuxedo with a row of medals pinned to the jacket. In one hand, he carried a carved walking stick. In the other was the top hat. He smiled as he placed it on his head and inspected his drum corps. Then he floated up and ran a white-gloved hand over the top of the window trim. Dust smudged his fingertip, and he shook his head at Emily. She spun onto her other side, away from him. The curtains billowed again. The old man approached the bed and bent down toward Emily. She sat upright, waking herself up with a shout. "Go away!"

Emily looked around the room. Other than her sleeping husband, it was empty.

| Sam woke to streaks of daylight falling across his face. He eased himself out of bed so as not to wake Emily. The first thing he saw was the top hat sitting on the dresser by the door. Why would she bring that thing upstairs with her? He headed for the bathroom.

Twenty minutes later, Sam hurried into the kitchen and filled his thermos with coffee. Emily sat at the table, yawning into her mug.

"I'm gone. Early site meeting this morning." He kissed the top of her head. "You sleep okay?"

"Fine. You?"

"Like a rock."

He disappeared out the door. A second later, he was back. "What's on the gourmet menu tonight?"

Emily gave him a blank look.

"Amateur chef's club? Dinner for eight? Tonight. Seven o'clock. It's our turn."

Emily gasped. "Crap. I totally forgot. Are you sure it's tonight? Not next week?"

"Tonight's the night, babe. Don't worry. I'll come home early to help."

"You? In the kitchen? Cooking?"

"Stranger things have happened."

And he was gone again.

| Emily's bulging book bag was heavy on her shoulder. She held the bundle of essays in one hand and a go-mug of coffee in the other as she wove her way through a throng of students and professors rushing to get to class on time.

Ahead, above the crowd, Emily caught a glimpse of a black top hat. On the tips of her toes, she strained to see where it went, but too many people blocked her view. A moment later, she saw the hat again as it turned a corner.

"Get a grip, Em," she muttered, taking a flight of stairs to her classroom.

Half an hour later, Emily sensed that her students were as weary of listening to her voice as she was of talking. She put aside her notes, sat on the desk, and kicked off her shoes.

"I think we need a little change of pace. Let's do some informal writing."

Everyone in the class groaned. Emily continued. "It's a good writing exercise. Jumping jacks for your brains."

Several students said they couldn't think of anything to write about.

"I'll give you a word." She picked up a marker and wrote "UNCANNY" on the whiteboard.

"Write about what 'uncanny' means to you. Anything it brings to mind. Don't stop to think or edit yourselves. Whatever comes into your head. Keep your pen moving across the page. We'll go for ten minutes."

Emily put her shoes back on and wandered through the aisles, watching her students spill their thoughts. She was pleased with her impromptu word choice. Despite their initial resistance, they were writing. A few phrases caught her eye as she walked around, some repeated on several pages: "something weird"; "makes me shiver"; "probably a hallucination."

Emily paused in front of the window. Outside, a few students lounged on the benches in the square below. Others lay on the grass. Two tossed a frisbee back and forth. When a black top hat flew by the window, Emily rubbed her eyes and pressed her forehead onto the glass for a closer look. Nothing.

| Sam poured the wine as Emily served caprese salad to their guests. He liked having people in his home, got a high from the energy he felt as a host, relished making people laugh.

"I've been cooking all day," Sam said to a series of good-natured guffaws.

"Great salad, Emily."

"We know Sam had nothing to do with it."

"Right you are," said Sam. "My girl did it all. Here's to you, babe."

They all raised their glasses to Emily. Sam was pleased to see her smile. His wife's serious book face, the one he'd seen too much of lately, turned impish when she smiled. Maybe this evening with friends would relax her.

"You look great, Sue," Sam said. "Pregnancy suits you. Doesn't Sue look great, Em?"

"Absolutely terrific."

Emily was grateful that she could retreat into the kitchen at this point. Among this group of friends, all past thirty-five, first pregnancies had become an epidemic. She found all small talk exhausting, but none more than pregnancy chatter. She was content to step away and leave Sam to work his charm.

Maybe if he poured enough wine into their friends, they might not notice that the evening's entrée didn't fit the definition of a gourmet meal. The water came to a boil, and she added pasta and waited for it to soften. Occasionally, voices called out to her as she stirred the pot.

"Em, did you hear about the Bannermans? Twins!"

Twins. Yikes. Emily tossed the steaming pasta with olive oil and bottled marinara sauce, then reached for the Italian parsley and organic basil she'd picked up at the market on her way home.

"Need any help in there?"

"No, I'm nearly done," she said, in her best happy-hostess voice. She sprinkled the chopped herbs over the pasta and hefted the loaded platter. The door between the kitchen and the dining room had swung shut, so she backed through, pushing the door with her butt. "Sam, you really need to level this door..."

She turned to see everyone in the room wearing a black top hat. Emily dropped the platter and threw her hands over her face. When they fell away a few moments later, seven pairs of eyes stared back at her in shocked silence. Not a top hat in sight.

| Sam watched the platter plummet, felt it shatter on the floor, saw the shock on Emily's face. What the hell? He glanced around the table at their guests, who seemed frozen in their seats, unsure of what to do.

"I must have tripped," said Emily, bending down to start picking up the debris.

In a few quick strides, Sam was beside his wife, pulling her up, steadying her with his arm, and laughing. "We planned that, folks! The evening's entertainment. Next up is Emily's dancing mop, followed by her famous robotic vacuum cleaner."

"Shame on you, Sam," said Sue. "Emily's not a dancing mop."

"And she's certainly not a robotic vacuum," said another woman. "Poor Emily. She looks like she's seen a ghost."

"He didn't mean it like that," said one of the guys.

"You women are so sensitive," chided another.

The words continued to spill out, voices talking over each other, rising. Sam glanced at Emily, who was staring down at the fragments of platter in her hands. He felt her shiver and tightened his arm around her shoulder.

"Let's all settle down. Ladies, please excuse my sad attempt at humour. Em, are you all right?"

She nodded.

"See? Ghosts don't scare her," said Sam. "She's a Shakespeare expert."

"You look pale, Emily. I think we should go," said Sue.

"No way," said Sam. "I'll open another bottle of wine and order some pizza."

| Emily was restless in her sleep again that night. The drum corps appeared at the end of the bed, followed by Grandfather Sir. He stepped gingerly over Sam's socks and brushed his dusty jeans aside with the toe of his polished dress shoe.

Then Emily was beside him at the window. The street below transformed into a field of wheat, where a little girl sat alone. Then they were down beside the girl. They all waded through a bumper crop of grain. In a clearing, they came upon a ragtag ensemble: a tired nun, a society matron wearing a string of pearls, a dishevelled businessman holding a cocktail glass, a long-haired hippie in a tie-dyed bandana, and a teenage boy covered with tattoos. Everyone carried a baby.

With Emily at his side, Grandfather Sir marched down the lineup, tapping each one on the head with his walking stick. When he came to the little girl, a glass bowl containing a single goldfish appeared in her hands. Grandfather Sir raised the goldfish bowl high in the air with the end of his stick. The bowl exploded. Feathers floated down. The wheat grew up around them.

| Sam wasn't sure what woke him up, but he was alone in the bed. Emily was huddled in the corner by the window, wearing the hat. Sam got out of bed and tiptoed over to Emily. She hadn't had a sleepwalking episode for several years, but he remembered not to startle her. Even so, when he tapped her shoulder, she jumped.

"You killed my fish!"

Sam pulled Emily to her feet and led her back to bed. He tossed the hat back onto the dresser.

"That's it. First thing in the morning, I'm taking that thing to the dump."

"No. I need to keep it."

"You need to get some sleep."

"The hat is haunting me."

"That's crap. You had a nightmare. Probably something you ate—the pepperoni on the pizza."

They lay in the dark, staring at the ceiling. After a few minutes, Sam turned on his side. "Go to sleep, Em."

"Sam, do you have dreams?"

"If I do, I have the good sense not to remember them."

| The next morning, Emily sat curled up in an overstuffed armchair, spilling out her hat stories.

"It sounds like you have a purposeful ghost on your hands."

Emily shook her head. " That's crazy, Katherine. I don't believe in ghosts. Besides, if a ghost was going to haunt me, wouldn't it be Dad, not Grandfather?"

"Maybe suicides don't get to be ghosts."

Emily put her left hand on her belly and massaged her churning gut, aware that Katherine was watching her.

" That's not funny, Kay."

"Sorry. I'm listening."

" That hat has triggered something. I don't know how to stop it."

" You can't stop it. You have to understand it."

"I don't know what's real and what's not anymore."

" Try writing your grandfather a letter."

" A letter? What for?"

" To say how you feel. Come on, Em. You're a teacher. You know what for."

"And where should I send this damn letter? P.O. Box Hell?"

"Sending it doesn't matter. Writing it is what counts."

"I'm not writing a letter to my dead grandfather."

"He may be an apparition, but you have to deal with him somehow."

On her way home from class, Emily stopped for groceries. Standing at the end of one aisle was Grandfather Sir, pointing his stick at her. *I'm not falling for this. I don't see anything. He's not there.* She moved to the next aisle. So did he. Same with the next. And the next. Emily abandoned her grocery buggy in the last aisle and went home.

| That afternoon, for the second time in less than twenty-four hours, Sam woke Emily with a tap on the shoulder. This time

she was slumped across her desk, an unfinished letter open on her computer screen.

"Hey you. It's dinnertime, not bedtime. What are you writing?"

"A letter to my grandfather."

"Why?"

"A suggestion from Katherine. I saw her this afternoon."

"Great. And how is our friendly neighbourhood shrink?"

"She's not a shrink, Sam. She's a. . ."

". . .psychologist, therapist, analyst, whatever. They're all shrinks."

Emily slammed her laptop shut.

Sam stepped back. "Okay. I know she's your best friend. What else did she have to say?"

"Not much."

"Like hell."

"You won't like it."

"If it helps you get some sleep, I'll like it a lot."

"She said it's a disturbance, a manifestation. It could be from stress or lack of sleep. Or unresolved anxieties, or latent anger, or the ticking time bomb that is my so-called biological clock, or my superego fighting for control of my id."

Sam leaned against the door. "Terrific. Can you take a pill for that?"

"She also said it might be about you and me."

| Wearing one of Emily's aprons, Sam stood at the kitchen sink slicing mushrooms. Nearby, a pan of chopped onions sizzled on the stove. He grinned in Emily's direction.

"Are you sure I have to learn to cook?"

Emily grinned back at him.

"If you want us to stay in that silly gourmet club, you do."

"Am I going to have to do it a lot?"

"Every single day. I never want to buy bottled marinara sauce again. We'll make a big batch tonight and freeze it."

Emily picked up the pile of broken platter pieces still lying on the counter where she'd left them. "I can't quite bring myself to throw these out."

Sam took them from her and threw the pieces in the garbage. "There. Problem solved."

"Damn. I liked that platter," said Emily.

"And I liked the hundred bucks I spent last night ordering pizza for eight people."

Emily peered at the platter shards in the garbage can. "I could probably find another one just like it on eBay."

"No more eBay for you."

Sam stood back to admire his pile of chopped mushrooms. "How's this?"

"Smaller pieces. And more onions."

Emily went to the sink to wash her hands. Out the window, Grandfather Sir stood in the back yard. He smiled at her, touched his walking stick to his hat, and gave a slight bow. She flung the curtains shut.

"What's the matter?" asked Sam.

"Not a thing."

He opened the curtains and saw nothing but dusk. "Something spooked you."

"I saw him again."

"If you mean your grandfather, he was a stuffy old fart. And he's dead. Forget about him."

"He won't let me."

Sam moved to Emily's side and raised her chin. "Stay busy. Think of other things. Like going upstairs...making that baby we've been talking about..."

"You've been talking about."

Sam danced Emily around the room and whispered in her ear: "You'll be a great mother."

Emily stopped dancing. "What does that mean?"

Sam looked puzzled. "It means you'll naturally do all the things that good mothers naturally do."

"But what does it mean for me?"

"Huh?"

"That's what I mean. You don't get it. That's a question I'm not even supposed to ask."

"But isn't that what women want, to be good mothers?"

"What is it with men? You have to fit all women into the mother box. What kind of box should we put you into?"

Sam took off the apron and headed for the door. "That's it. End of cooking lesson."

"Sam, leaving the room every time we get to something you don't want to talk about isn't a solution."

"What's to talk about? I want a kid. You don't."

"It's not that I don't. It's that it will affect my life more than yours."

"You don't know that. We'll be in it together. I'm not your grandfather. And I'm certainly not your father. I'm not going to jump off a bridge."

Now it was Emily's turn to head for the door.

Sam's fist hit the counter. "So I can't leave the room, but you can. Go. Run back to your desk and your damned marking. Have you ever figured out how much you make an hour after ten years of university? Probably less than fifty cents. That fucking place won't ever offer you a real job. Why do you let them use you like slave labour?"

Emily stepped back. "I think you're still mad because I didn't take your name when we got married."

"Em, how many times do I have to say this? I get it. It's fine. Goodwin is easier than Christopoulos. I should change my name to yours."

"Then why do I feel this undercurrent of anger from you?"

"We had a plan. Buy a house. Done. Save some money. Done. Try for a baby. Not done. You've changed the plan. And now you've flipped out. What the hell happened, Em?"

"I don't know."

"It's that goddamn hat."

"You might be right. Maybe I'll drive down to the river and throw it off the train bridge."

"Bad idea. That bridge has bad family karma for you."

"Time to change the karma. Grandfather built that bridge. It's a perfect place to get rid of his hat. Besides, not many trains cross there anymore."

"Absolutely not. Let me bury the stupid thing in a bed of concrete tomorrow morning. I guarantee it'll never bother you again."

"No. Whatever I decide, I have to do myself. Stir the onions before they burn, and add the mushrooms. Please."

Sam waved the spatula at Emily. "I don't want you anywhere near that bridge."

| That night, after two hours at her desk, Emily had marked only three essays, each worse than the last. One C– and two Ds. Each

D grade made her feel like a failure. She took another from the pile as Sam emerged from the kitchen.

"The cooking part's okay. But the cleaning up is a drag."

Emily nodded without looking up from her desk.

"Are you coming up?"

"In half an hour. I want to do at least one more."

Sam left. Emily felt a strong urge to go on eBay, but she restrained herself and checked her email instead. Nine messages from students complaining that she hadn't returned their essays yet. Her head fell into her hands.

The phone rang. Emily looked at the clock. Almost midnight. It could only be one person. "Hi Mom…no, I'm not asleep yet…Yes, I got the hat…No, please don't send the war medals. The hat is more than enough…No, I'm not pregnant yet. We're not even sure if…yes. I know I'm not getting any younger. Good night, Mom."

An hour later, Emily slipped into bed beside Sam. Every time her eyes began to close, she heard the faint sound of drums. This went on for hours, with Emily jolting awake each time she fell asleep. Finally, she threw off the covers.

| Emily sat in her car until the first rays of sunlight hit the top of the bridge, rendering the rusty steel girders a deep orange. With the hat tucked under her arm, she walked to the rails. Far below, the river was calm in the still morning air. Emily moved to the middle of the bridge and stood on the tracks. She wound up and hurled the hat as high into the sky as she could.

The hat carved a boomerang loop over the water, returned to the bridge, and landed right-side-up on the tracks not far from where she stood.

She scowled at the hat. "How do I get rid of you?"

Emily's feet felt the vibrations before the train whistle blew. She vaulted over the rail and dropped onto a small platform attached to the side of the bridge. A rush of air swooshed dust onto her as she covered her head with one arm and wrapped the other around the railing. The bridge shook and rattled so violently, Emily thought it would fly apart. The train seemed endless. When it finally cleared the bridge, she climbed back onto the tracks and watched the caboose recede. Grandfather Sir was standing on it, his hand raised in a salute.

When the train had disappeared, Emily looked back over the bridge. The hat was still there. She peered both ways before returning to the rails to pick it up. It was dusty and bent, but otherwise intact. She wound up to fling it into the water again, but stopped. For the first time in months, she felt calm. She put the hat on her head and strolled back to her car.

| Sam had looked everywhere. She was gone. Her car was gone. The hat was gone. That damn bridge. He dressed in a rush, grabbed his car keys, and was opening the garage door when Emily pulled into the driveway.

"You scared the crap out of me, Em. You went to the bridge, didn't you?"

"Yes."

"Did you dump the hat?"

"Tried to." She pulled it from the back seat of her car. "But it wouldn't let me."

"This ends today. Give me that thing."

"No. It can stay." Emily put the hat on her head. "It's fine. The ghost is gone."

"How do you know?"

She put her hands up to his face. He put his hands on her shoulders.

"Answer me, Em. How do you know your ghost is gone?"

"He took the last train out of town. I'm okay now."

Later that day, Sam and Emily packed the top hat into the box, tied it tight with string, and placed it on the highest shelf in the storage room. That night they slept soundly. Neither one stirred when Grandfather Sir appeared, alone, no honour guard, no ragtag ensemble. He inspected the room, pulled the blanket up over Emily's shoulder, and whispered in her ear.

"I'll be back. Next time I'll bring your father. It'll be fun."

Estate Planning

FIVE MONTHS after his wife Harriet's funeral, Lorne Sawchuk should not have been surprised when his youngest daughter announced that she'd dropped out of school. Although he was against this move, Lorne didn't pressure Laura—she wasn't thinking clearly, she missed her mother, she'd change her mind. After all, graduation was only a few months away. He decided to leave her alone, giving her time and space to reconsider. For two days, she didn't come out of her room.

On the third morning, when Laura appeared with her backpack over her shoulder, Lorne was relieved. He watched as she boarded the school bus and waved as it receded down the road, pleased that he'd handled the situation without getting riled up. But that afternoon, when the same bus drove past without stopping at the end of their driveway, his gut began to churn.

In the heavy quiet of his kitchen that evening, Lorne ate his dinner of canned stew and convinced himself that Laura must be spending the night at a friend's house, and had simply forgotten to let him know. The next forty-eight hours passed with still no word from her, so Lorne drove to the school. The principal pulled up his daughter's attendance record.

"Since her mother passed, Laura has missed at least three days of classes every week. We tried to contact you."

"How?"

"We sent notes home with Laura."

"I didn't get them."

"We realized that, so we sent letters by mail. We got no response."

"Laura picks up the mail each day."

"I phoned the house twice, at supper time, and got no answer."

"I was in my barn. There's no phone out there."

Lorne went to the police station and filed a missing persons report. The officer said they'd watch out for her, but that runaways were hard to locate, especially if they didn't want to be found. Besides, Laura would be eighteen in the fall. Almost an adult.

For the next month, Lorne drove to every nearby town looking for his daughter. He even went into the city, where he walked through crowded malls and dark smoky bars, finding no trace of Laura.

Lorne called Toronto. "It's been almost six weeks now, Richard. I don't know where else to look for her. Could you come out here?"

"I'm overloaded right now, Dad. In the middle of a big case. There's huge money involved and a famous client. I can't reveal who, so don't ask. My advice is to stop looking. Laura's always been a wild little thing. You and Mom spoiled her. She'll come home when she's hungry enough. I know that sounds harsh, but it's time for some tough love."

Lorne called Vancouver next. "She still hasn't come home, Susan. Are you sure you have no idea where she might be?"

"I wish I knew, Dad, but Laura was a little kid when I left home. I don't know who her friends are now, or where she hangs out."

"Maybe you could come out for a few days?"

"Aw, Dad. I'm so busy with the girls. Olivia and Zoe have gymnastics classes and their dance lessons. And Ava has two play-dates scheduled this week. Peter's no help. He's working twelve-hour days at the clinic, and is on call every second weekend. I can't get away."

"I understand."

"I know you're worried. And Mom would be beside herself, with her precious baby missing. Try to relax. Laura's flexing her wings. She'll come home when she's ready. Let me know when you hear from her. In the meantime, look after yourself."

For the first time in his life, Lorne didn't know what to do. He yearned for Harriet's counsel and knew she wouldn't stop searching until she found her daughter. So, despite Richard and Susan's advice, he kept going, driving from town to town, carrying a picture of Laura with him. During that time, he talked to more strangers than he had in his entire life. At night, he slept on Harriet's side of the bed.

At the mailbox cluster one afternoon, Lorne was fumbling for his key when a girl pulled up beside him in a truck, opened the driver's window, and waved her arm out at him.

"Hi, Mr. Sawchuk. How's it going?"

"Fine, thanks. And yourself?" said Lorne. He had no idea who this person was.

"Good. Have you heard from Laura?"

Lorne grabbed the girl's arm. "No. Have you? Do you know where she is?"

She shook her head. "She started going with a guitar player. His band got some gigs and hit the road. Laura went with them. You're hurting my arm."

Lorne let go. "Sorry. What's the guitar player's name?"

"I'm not sure—Curt, maybe. Or Clint? Kyle?"

"And the band?"

" They didn't have a name yet."

"If you hear from my daughter, please call me."

With a leaden ache in his chest, Lorne stopped searching and went back to his barn.

| After two years of travelling with the band, Laura was tired. She'd earned her keep: been part of the crew, a roadie lugging amps from the van to backstage doors, running cable, listening to the same off-key set night after night, then packing it all up and repeating in the next town, the next city, the next province. She and her boyfriend stayed in cheap motels when they had gigs, and slept in the van when they didn't.

One night, he brought two giggling girls back to their hotel room. "Hey babe, Heidi and Holly are going to bunk in here tonight, and head out with us tomorrow."

"Are you serious? Look at them. They can't be more than fourteen."

" Take it or leave it, sugar. Your choice."

Laura slept on a bench in a city park for one night, her long hair tucked up under a cap. By the next morning, she knew she didn't have the courage to survive alone on the streets. All that day, she wandered around, moving from one coffee shop to another. What now? Christ, what now?

That evening, at a bar the band had once played, she ran into the drummer's ex-girlfriend.

"I remember you. Laura, right?"

Laura nodded. "Hi Annie. I missed you when you left."

"I couldn't stand it anymore."

"I'm done too."

"Where're you staying?"

"The nearest park bench."

"That's not safe. I've got a couch."

The next morning, Annie mentioned that the coffee shop she worked at was hiring. Laura went for an interview and was handed an apron.

The following week, Laura didn't feel well. She went to a drop-in clinic and asked for some 'flu medicine. "When was your last period?" asked the doctor.

That afternoon, Laura climbed out the apartment's only window and crouched on the twelfth-floor ledge. Soon a small crowd gathered in the parking lot below, pointing up. Laura looked down, got dizzy, and pressed herself hard against the ledge. She closed her eyes. Her mother's face floated through her mind. Then a flash of her mother's body, lying crumpled between the house and the barn, beside a tray of spilled coffee and cookies scattered in the dirt.

Laura opened her eyes. Down below, she saw Annie get off a bus and run into their building. Two minutes later, Annie was leaning out the window, reaching her hand towards Laura. Laura didn't move.

"You've been so nice, Annie. Thank you. But I'm very tired."

"Listen to me. You'll get through this. I know what I'm talking about. That jerk isn't worth your life."

"I don't care about him."

"You must care about somebody." Annie leaned out farther. This time, Laura did take her hand.

A few days later, Annie accompanied Laura to a different clinic.

| When Lorne saw his daughter standing on the doorstep, he pulled her inside and wrapped his arms around her. They stood like that for several minutes. Lorne already knew that he wouldn't ask any questions about the last two years—that night or ever. He carried her backpack upstairs and opened the door to her room.

"It might be a little dusty."

Lorne had left it exactly the way it had been on the day she disappeared. Even her chemistry book was still open on the desk.

Laura slept for three days. Each morning, Lorne stood outside her bedroom door and called her name. When she didn't answer, he went in, walked over to her bed, and placed his hand on her forehead. Before going out to the barn, he brought her tea and toast. Each evening, he checked on her before retiring for the night, and left a plate of cheese beside her bed.

Four mornings later, Laura got up before her father. She showered and went down to the kitchen where she made breakfast for two, complete with eggs, bacon, and hash browns. When Lorne walked in, he kissed her forehead and took his seat at the table. They ate in silence.

"Best breakfast ever. Next to your mother's, of course," said Lorne as he left for the barn.

| Alone in the kitchen, Laura expected her mother to walk in at any moment. Three years had passed since Harriet's death, yet her presence filled each cupboard and drawer. Her teakettle still sat on the same element of the stove. Lorne never used the kettle. He was a coffee man.

Although the room looked the same, it was also dusty and somewhat rundown, a condition Harriet would never have tolerated. Laura spent the next week restoring it to her mother's standards. She scrubbed the appliances, floors, and countertops; cleaned out the cupboards and sponged the walls; took down the curtains and washed them. Then she patched cracks and painted walls, using the same sky blue her mother had picked out over three decades ago. She rehung the curtains and stood back to admire her work. Harriet's kitchen sparkled.

Only one part remained untouched: the pantry. Harriet's cookbooks filled three shelves. Laura pulled them off and piled them on the kitchen table. After wiping down all the pantry shelves, Laura sat in her mother's chair and went through each book, page by page, pausing for long minutes when she found fingerprints and thumb marks on the paper, Harriet's identifying whorls captured in blueberry juice or chocolate sauce. Laura ran her fingers over the pencilled-in margin notes that said "yummy," or "too much sugar," or "very good with cashews added," or "make again, Laura likes it."

Harriet had been a skilled all-round cook, but her specialty was baking. In a bulging red-and-white box held shut with a piece of ribbon, Laura found her mother's baking recipes, each on an index card, ingredients printed clearly in capital letters, instructions written in her mother's tidy hand. Laura counted the cards: fifty-seven recipes, for everything from plain white bread to black forest cake. She held the box up to her nose. It smelled like gingersnap cookies. Laura tied the ribbon back around the box and returned it to the pantry.

The next morning, the red-and-white box was back on the kitchen table.

"Did you move this from the pantry, Dad?"

"No. Haven't seen that since..."

Laura put it away.

The morning after that, the red-and-white box was again back on the kitchen table. Again, she asked her father if he'd moved it. Again, the answer was negative.

"Do have any trouble with sleepwalking, Dad?"

"No. I wake up in the same position as I was when I crawled into bed the night before."

Laura left the box on the table all day. Every time she walked into the room, she stopped to look at it. A plan took shape in her mind. She'd bake her way through this box. She'd recreate all Harriet's baking recipes. If she messed one up, she'd make it again until she got it right.

The first few days of this experiment resulted in more than a few disasters. Unkneadable doughs and stringy batters ended up in the garbage, along with burned muffins and dinner rolls that refused to rise. But by the week's end, Laura felt Harriet's enthusiasm for confectionary creation come alive in her flour-covered hands. Soon the kitchen counters overflowed with the results of Laura's efforts. The aromas drew Lorne in from the barn earlier and more often.

As she worked, especially when kneading dough, Laura's mind wandered. Sometimes she wondered about her baby—him or her. Herm. Who would "herm" have been? Would she have had an abortion if she could have come home to her mother? Would she ever forget? She didn't come up with any answers, but began to feel more comfortable with the questions.

Laura and Lorne couldn't eat everything she made, so she started selling her baking at the local market every Saturday morning. Soon a nearby groceteria asked for regular deliveries of her breads and cakes. Within a few months, she was making a profit.

One day after lunch, as Lorne walked from the house back to the barn, Laura saw him clutch his heart and fall to the ground. She dialed 911, then ran to her father and thumped his chest.

| The doctors told Lorne that he'd recover, but would never farm again. Along with the heart attack, he'd had a stroke and would need time in a rehabilitation hospital. After that, he'd need a lot of help, either at home or in an extended care centre. Looking at Laura, the doctors recommended extended care.

A week after their father's heart attack, Richard and Susan arrived. In Lorne's hospital room, the family discussed options for the future. Or rather, Richard and Susan had a discussion, while Lorne and Laura listened.

Susan was earnest and practical. " You should sell everything and move close to me, Dad. Then I could visit you every weekend. And I'm sure my girls would find time to drop by. You'd get to know your granddaughters."

Richard had another plan. " You should definitely come to Toronto. One of my clients owns a high-end seniors' residence. I talked to him about a spot for you. I travel a lot, but I'd visit when I'm in town."

Lorne shook his head. "I'm not going anywhere."

"Neither am I," said Laura.

Richard and Susan returned to Toronto and Vancouver. Laura visited her father at the hospital every day. And she wasn't alone. Laura had always thought of her father as a solitary man, but he and Harriet had made many friends in their years together. His room filled with get-well cards and bright coloured balloons. When a neighbour offered to lease Lorne's land, he accepted.

Another friend owned a small house on the edge of the city, not far from the farm. It was empty. "I'll sell it to you, Lorne, for a good price. Two bedrooms on one floor, no stairs."

When Lorne was discharged from the hospital, he and Laura moved into the bungalow. Laura was concerned that her father would miss his barn. Lorne was concerned that Laura would miss her mother's kitchen. They were both right. But they adapted. Laura got a job at the local bakery, and took her father out to his barn for a few hours every Sunday afternoon.

Three months later, when the bakery owner decided to retire, Lorne bought the business.

"I hope you didn't buy it because I work there, Dad."

"I bought it because it's a good investment."

Three months after that, with Laura as manager, the bakery profits were up by twenty-five per cent.

On good-weather days, when Laura came home from work, Lorne would be in his rocking chair on the porch. Sometimes he'd be asleep, so she'd tiptoe past him and set about preparing their supper. When it was ready, she'd call him in. One evening, he didn't respond. She went to the door and called again. *Dad?*

| Lorne's funeral was crowded. Farm neighbours and people from all the surrounding towns arrived in their pickup trucks. Richard gave a long and eloquent eulogy, during which Laura felt as if he was talking about someone she didn't know. Susan dabbed at her eyes throughout the service. Laura was dry-eyed. Crying was for the night, for the solitude of her bedroom.

At the reception after the funeral, Lorne's lawyer friend asked the siblings to meet at his office the next morning to discuss Lorne's will.

"I don't know what you're talking about. I have my father's will," said Richard. "He made it six months after Mother died."

"Now invalid," said the lawyer. "Your father made a new will last year."

The next morning, Richard, Susan, and Laura walked to the lawyer's office. The floor squeaked as they entered the old house. Overstuffed chairs surrounded a carved oak desk.

"This room looks like a 1950s movie set," said Susan.

The lawyer gestured to the chairs.

"Doesn't your provincial law association have a mandatory retirement age?" said Richard.

The lawyer ignored him and began the reading of their father's will. The estate was more substantial than any of his children had imagined, and Lorne had been thorough in assigning his assets. The farmland was to be sold to his neighbour for a pre-arranged price, and the money divided between Richard and Susan. Susan's daughters each received five hundred dollars. The rest of his estate—which included a sizable investment portfolio, the farmhouse, the barn, the bungalow, and the bakery—all went to Laura, who was also named her father's executor.

For several minutes, nothing moved in the room except for the lawyer's eyes shifting from Richard to Susan to Laura. Richard and Susan's faces had grown red. Laura's was white.

"I can see your fingerprints all over that will, Laura," said Susan.

"Laura had nothing to do with this will," said the lawyer.

"Bullshit," said Richard. " The little brat filled his head with what she wanted every day. He didn't know what he was doing."

The lawyer locked eyes with Richard as he spoke: " Your father decided the conditions of this will on his own. And his mind was sound."

The door slammed hard behind Richard.

Susan looked hard at Laura: "I hope you're happy." Then she followed her brother.

Laura didn't move. Susan's words bounced around in her head, but her mind was still stumbling over the word "executor." She pressed the palms of her hands together, rubbed them back and forth, brought them up to her face, and kneaded her forehead with her fingertips. Finally, she found her voice.

"I'm only twenty-two. I didn't finish high school. I don't know anything about estates and executors."

She could see the old lawyer's eyes above the rim of his glasses.

" Your father had great confidence in you, my dear."

| The customer stood at the cash register in Laura's bakery, holding a brown paper bag of granola. He smiled at Laura.

"It's for my mom."

"Good choice. It's a fresh batch. I made it last night."

He handed her a ten-dollar bill. " You look familiar. Do you live around here?"

Laura also thought she'd seen him before. " Three streets over. I moved in just over six months ago. Do you need a bag for that?"

He shook his head and stuffed the granola into his backpack. As he turned to leave, a pair of lime-green running shoes tied to his pack caught Laura's eye. "Nice shoes. Are you a runner?"

"Yes. I try to get a run in every day."

"Where?"

"Mostly out near my grandfather's farm."

"Range Road 22?" said Laura.

"How'd you know?"

"That's where I've seen you. I grew up on Range Road 30. The Sawchuk place."

"White barn with green trim?"

"Yes. I spend every Sunday out there. Just started running myself."

"Go for a run sometime?" he said. "I'll give you some tips."

He looked like an athlete. Laura wasn't sure she was ready for that. "I don't know. I'm slow and I work six days a week."

He looked at the schedule posted beside the door. "But you're closed on Sundays. How about noon? Meet at the mailboxes?"

Laura nodded.

His face creased into a warm, wide grin. "Great. My name's Will. See you Sunday."

"Will," said Laura. "You're not a musician, are you?"

"Nope. Can't play a note. But I can dance."

| Laura touched the arm of the rocking chair as she crossed the porch. "Hi, Dad. I sold out of my new granola recipe again today."

She changed into shorts and a T-shirt. Over the last few weeks, since that day in the lawyer's office, she'd taken up running. She wasn't sure why, other than her legs told her they needed to move.

She laced up her shoes, telling herself to run first and check her email when she got back. But that damn computer was a magnet. Laura scanned her inbox, hoping not to find anything new from her siblings. *They must be too busy to harass me today.*

As if on cue, two emails popped up, one from Richard saying that he'd launched a legal challenge to Lorne's will. The other was from Susan: "I'm sorry. Can we talk sometime?" Laura deleted Richard's message and responded "Yes" to Susan's.

Then she pulled a baseball cap onto her head and started a slow jog down the street. Her legs felt strong and steady. She'd go long today. A training run before Sunday.

The Ballad of Jake and Janet

BLISS IS AN UNTRUSTWORTHY EMOTION. Jake Smart didn't know that as he listened to the party and gazed at the lake. A host of midnight boaters cruised the shimmering water, more than usual on this calm night. Surely they'd want to drift closer to the fun, drawn by the music, the cabin's blazing lights, the silhouettes of dancing couples cast high on the cedar walls. Low in the ebony sky, the Big Dipper's corners rose above the horizon and shone bright against the dark, a waxing gibbous moon rising steadily into the cloudless atmosphere.

Jake was surrounded by friends. His longtime buddies lounged against the deck railings or drifted down to the beach bonfire.

"Hey Jakey! Saw the new wheels out front. What year is it?"

Jake raised his beer in his friend's direction. "A '92. Brand new. Drove it off the showroom floor two days ago."

"Swank."

When the word "bliss" ran through his mind, Jake was surprised. It wasn't a typical thought for him. But there it was, a perfect match for the song coming through the patio speakers. Rising violin crescendos swept Robert Plant's honey-dripping voice far over the water, its silky cadence melding with the air.

Jake knew it was a sappy song, but he didn't care. He liked it.
He listened, hummed, and breathed it all in. And bliss. He liked
that, too.

Jake reached for his wife's hand, but Janet pulled it away and
slid her fingers into her pocket. He slipped his other arm around
her waist. She wriggled away.

"Lighten up, J. Let's dance."

"No."

Jake watched her walk down to the water's edge. After ten
years, he still craved her petite body, trim hips unaffected by
three pregnancies. They'd been kids when they got married. His
father had done everything he could to talk him out of it.

"So she's knocked up. We can handle that a different way.
You're only eighteen. Don't get married. It's a trap. You'll be
bored in months."

Jake liked that his father had been wrong. Tonight, he
wanted Janet to feel what he did, this deep happiness, this ideal
moment on an ideal night. He lifted the cooler lid, pulled out
two cans of beer, and joined her on the dock. He rolled a cold
one up Janet's arm. She took the can and snapped it open at the
same time as Jake opened his. They both took deep swigs and
sank down onto the dock's wide-planked surface. A hundred
moons rippled across the water. Jake swept his arm across
the view.

"Look at this." He touched his head to his wife's shoulder.
"What a night. What a place to be."

"Yes, it's beautiful. And yes, I still want to move."

"But we grew up here."

"This town is stifling us, Jake."

"I don't feel stifled."

"Your father is stifling us."

"Our home is here, J."

"We'll make a home in the city. It'll be good for the kids."

"It won't be the same."

"Different can be good, Jake."

"This lake is in my blood."

"This lake killed your mother."

"My mother killed my mother. The lake was an innocent bystander."

They sat in silence for a moment, the water lapping at the dock's footings beneath them.

"I still think we should have named one of the girls Isobel," said Janet. "Your mother would have liked that."

Jake shook his head. "I'm glad we didn't. Kids need their own names. Free of baggage."

Robert Plant's voice filled the air once more. *Come...*

"There's our song again. How can you resist? Let's dance."

"Okay, but we're not done with this."

They walked up the hill, hand-in-hand. Friends called out to them as they went.

"J and J! Looking good."

"Hey Jake! I see that Daddy bought you some sweet new wheels again. You lucky dog."

Jake waved his buddy away and led Janet into a gliding pattern of exaggerated waltz-like steps. As they moved, he sang into her hair, crooning the lyrics to "Sea of Love," words about the day they met, the day he knew she was his pet, the day he wanted her to be with him forever. He felt her resistance dissipate. She allowed him to guide her feet. He pulled her closer.

"Honey, you're off-key," she said. "But don't stop." Her head fell into his chest, muffling her words. They swayed together until the last notes of the song melted away. With a flourish, Jake bent his wife backward into a deep dip and whispered in her ear: "Let's get another beer."

"Aw, Jake. It's late. Sara was upset when we left this afternoon. I promised the girls we'd be at your father's place before they wake up in the morning."

"And we will be. One more beer. Then we'll go."

The eastern sky showed signs of dawn's light when Jake and Janet finally slid into their shiny red Corvette. Jake had taken it home the day it arrived at the dealership, laughing at himself all the way. He knew that restraint wasn't his most prominent character trait. One day, he'd have to learn how to say no to himself. After all, he was almost thirty now.

"This is a ridiculous vehicle for a man with three children," said Janet, as she settled down into the passenger seat. "But it's comfortable." She relaxed into the leather, sighed back into the headrest.

Jake guided the car along the road, feeling the breeze in his hair, humming the song that still resonated in his head. He pictured his three daughters asleep in their beds. His girls. They were more than enough for him. He didn't need a son. He had enough trouble being one. Maybe Janet was right. Maybe they did need some distance from this town. But a new start would require a new job, and he'd never worked for anyone but his father. He wondered if he could. Maybe it was time to find out.

"You win, J. We'll move. I'll tell Dad this weekend."

No answer. Jake glanced over at his sleeping wife and smiled. Tomorrow. They'd think about it again tomorrow. Tonight was for bliss.

The curves around the lake rolled together in a rhythmic dance—one segued from the last to the next, like a melody, a hypnotic lulling ride. Along the edge of a rising bluff, where the narrow road twisted into a hairpin turn that began a long spill into town, Jake's Corvette left the asphalt and soared over the water toward the fading moon.

| The double funeral took place on a steamy July day. Mourners streamed into town from every direction. The congregation filled the small church and overflowed into the yard. People shuffled their feet as they listened to the service, broadcast to those outside over crackling speakers fastened under the eaves.

In the front pew, Jacob Smart wore a heavy black suit. On the bench beside him was his grey fedora, a tiny peacock feather adorning the brim. Next to the hat, Jacob's three granddaugh-ters sat on the hard wood, lined up according to age, each wearing a grey long-sleeved frock with a white lace collar, a black hair ribbon, and pristine white gloves on small hands. At the other end of the pew sat Mayor Watson, Janet's father. The grandfathers, both widowers, had not spoken to each other for fifteen years.

The overcrowded church soon grew hot. Men wiped their brows with handkerchiefs. Women fanned their faces with the service programs. Two people fainted and were carried outside to lie under the shade of an elm tree. Despite the heat, no one left the church or the yard. When the service ended, people pressed in closer around the church steps so they didn't miss the moment the orphaned girls and their grandfathers emerged into the sun's glare.

"Did they speak?"

" To each other? I doubt that."

The ride to the cemetery offered the family no relief because the vehicle's air-conditioning was broken. Sara rolled the window down as the car crept along the town's main street. She looked down Raintree Lane, where their house was. Her mother and father's house. Her house. With a FOR SALE sign out front. Already.

During the interment, the relentless sun beat down on those who gathered around the fresh holes, dug side-by-side in the graveyard. As the two coffins sank into the ground, three-year-old Melanie reached up to her biggest sister. Ten-year-old Sara lifted Mel and settled the little one onto her left hip. Five-year-old Abby wrapped her arms around Sara's waist.

That night, at Grandfather Smart's house, Sara listened at the top of the stairs.

"They're my granddaughters too, Jacob."

"That's why you can see them on Saturday mornings from nine to ten."

"I'll sue for joint custody."

"How? I know your financial situation."

"You're doing this because of Isobel."

"You're damned right I am. You're responsible for what happened."

"We're both responsible. Let's make peace."

"Get the fuck out of my house."

Back in their room, Abby and Mel were still awake when Sara tiptoed in. Mel's bottom lip quivered: "I want to go home." Sara put the cassette tape her mother had made, a mix of their parents' favourite songs, into her portable stereo. Back at home, the girls liked to dance in the living room before bedtime each night. Sara urged Abby and Mel onto their feet and they swayed together hand-in-hand for a few moments. Then they all climbed into the same bed. Robert Plant's honeyed voice lulled them to sleep: *Come with me...*

Big Luck Island

NO ONE KNEW how the island got its name. Some said it came from a long-dead fisherman who caught the biggest walleye on record one misty morning after he anchored his boat near the choppy entrance to No Luck Cove. When the big fish took the bait, it almost toppled the dozing angler into the lake. Others claimed the island got its name because it brought big luck to everyone who came here. The trouble with big luck, the old ones said, was that it could be big good or big bad.

Mary Ellen McIntyre slouched in a deckchair as Karen McIntyre, arms loaded with groceries and towels, walked past her youngest daughter's bad mood without a glance. Paula trotted behind their mother, carrying two suitcases. She stuck her tongue out at her sibling. Mary Ellen responded with a finger flip.

Why the hell did they always have to be the first ones at the lake? No other cottage people bothered showing up until June. But oh no, as soon as the ice was gone, as soon as they could get to this stupid place in their stupid boat, Mary Ellen's mother dragged them out to this puny island. It had only three cabins. Nobody came here—at least no one worth knowing, certainly no one from her Grade Seven class. They didn't even have Internet. She was completely cut off from everyone, stuck on this island every weekend until school was out, and after that, all of July and August. By the end of the summer, she'd have no friends left. Mary Ellen's spring and summer stretched out ahead of her like an empty forever.

Their cabin was almost at water level, a feature Mary Ellen's mother liked because it wasn't too far to walk from the dock to the porch when they carried in their supplies. And they had their own beach, Karen always reminded her daughters.

Mary Ellen was totally unimpressed with their beach. It wasn't very big, and the sand wasn't really sand, just small pebbles. Some had sharp pointy edges. Everyone who waded into the water had to wear rubber swim shoes. Last summer, on a hot August afternoon, Mary Ellen emerged from the lake with a bloodsucker attached to her leg. She screamed and jumped around on the dock until her father ripped the leechy thing off.

Mary Ellen's mother went berserk: " You're supposed to soak them away in salt water. You could have torn the skin off her leg, you goddamned idiot."

That was the last time Mary Ellen's father came to the lake. A month later, he moved out of their house in the city.

" That's enough pouting for one day, Mary Ellen. Get off your butt and help us."

" Too late, Mom," said Paula. " The boat's empty."

" Then you can walk this bundle of mail over to Mrs. Merriweather's place. Maybe the exercise will improve your mood."

Mary Ellen hauled herself out of the chair.

"Stay on the trail. We don't know what critters crossed over on the ice during the winter."

" Why make me go if it might be dangerous?"

" And on your way back, check the small cabin. Maybe Uncle Keith is here. No one has heard from him for a while."

"Aw, Mom. Do I have to? He's disgusting and weird."

Her mother pointed down the path. "Go."

Mary Ellen trudged off. The wind had picked up, so she stopped by the shed to grab a windbreaker. Hanging in their spots on the wall were the two fishing rods her father had bought them a few years ago. She probably wouldn't be using hers much this year. The only one who ever took her fishing was her father. Her mother didn't like fishing, and Paula never wanted to do anything but read one of her dumb books or suntan on the dock with her tummy rolls hanging over her itty-bitty bikini bottom. Ew.

She kicked at stones along the trail until she came to where the path divided. One fork looped down to No Luck Cove. The other rose up to a lookout, the highest point on the island, Mary Ellen's favourite part of the whole stupid place. Last year a pair of bald eagles built a nest high in a tall spruce tree down by the water. Her father bought one of Mrs. Merriweather's hand-painted wooden benches and carried it up to the lookout. Mary Ellen had gone to that bench every day to watch the eagles take turns incubating their eggs. One was slightly bigger than the other, but the birds looked like twins, with their bright white heads, enormous dark-brown wings, and fierce yellow beaks. Their routine fascinated Mary Ellen. One parent stayed on the nest while the other took off to find food. Then they'd switch places, so they each had time to soar. Soon two eaglet heads appeared above the brim of the nest. Only one of the babies learned to fly. The other one simply disappeared. Mary Ellen didn't want to know what happened to it.

Today, she could still see the nest from the trail. It looked empty. Mary Ellen crested the hill and saw that her bench was still there, a little more weathered than last fall. From here, if she turned in a slow full circle, she could see the whole island and beyond, over the water to the other islands nearby. She looked down toward No Luck Cove and the rundown shack her Uncle Keith called a cabin. Smoke drifted from the chimney. Damn.

Mrs. Merriweather's cottage was the oldest here. She and her husband had once owned the whole island, before they sold part of it to Mary Ellen's grandparents. Most of the residents shuttered their places after the Labour Day weekend, but Mrs. Merriweather stayed longer than anyone else, arriving as soon as the ice was off the lake in the spring and not leaving until after Thanksgiving weekend. The island was accessible by snowmobile in the off-season. Who would be dumb enough to come out here in the winter? Mary Ellen was thankful that her mother hated driving on winter highways.

Karen treated Mrs. Merriweather as part of the family. "You girls should think of her as a summer grandmother. The poor thing is all by herself. Can you imagine? She's alone so much, you'd think she didn't have any family. It's outrageous that her children don't visit their mother in a beautiful place like this, especially now that she's a widow."

Mary Ellen's mother often rambled on about how Mrs. Merriweather took up her husband's woodworking projects after his death. She carved the same "Welcome Neighbour" benches, and painted the same mailboxes with the same images of woodland creatures.

"It's as if the wife absorbed all her husband's talents through osmosis. Isn't it wonderful that she didn't let his tools sit gathering dust in a gloomy shed? Such honour for his life's work."

If honouring someone's life work was such a good thing, Mary Ellen wanted to ask her mother, why had she sold all her father's tools at a garage sale as soon as he moved out of the house?

Mary Ellen stashed the mail in Mrs. Merriweather's squirrel mailbox, and walked over to Uncle Keith's place. The door opened before she could knock.

"Hey, kid. I thought you guys might be out for May Long."

"Mom says no one has heard from you for a while."

"Do me a favour and tell her my place is all locked up."

Her uncle's words were slurry, and he was even skinnier than the last time Mary Ellen had seen him. His straggly hair and gaunt face made him look much older than thirty-seven. She took a step back to avoid the body odour that wafted her way. His skin looked yellow.

"Are you sick?"

"Nope."

A mangy mutt that looked like a cross between a retriever and a German shepherd bounded up the steps and licked Mary Ellen's hand.

"Hey. He likes you. Usually he growls at strangers."

Mary Ellen knelt down to pet the dog. "What's his name?"

"Trigger. Like Roy Rogers's horse."

"Who's Roy Rogers?"

Keith's shoulders sagged. "Never mind."

Mary Ellen heard growling, but it wasn't coming from Trigger. "We brought groceries if you need some food."

"Did you bring any booze?"

"Just the white wine Mom likes."

"Where's your dad?"

"In the city. The divorce is done."

"Yeah. I heard. You okay with that?"

She shrugged. "Nobody checked with me about it."

"Tough to be the kid. Hang in there."

"I think my dad has a girlfriend."

"Don't be mad at him."

"Who should I be mad at?"

"You better go now. I got things to do."

She looked back after a few steps. Keith was vomiting over the railing.

| Mary Ellen sauntered into the kitchen. Her mother asked about Mrs. Merriweather.

"She wasn't there."

"Really? I'm surprised. Did you knock?"

"You didn't tell me to knock. You told me to deliver the mail. I put it in the squirrel."

"I hope she comes tomorrow. I miss her."

"And Uncle Keith? Do you miss him?"

"Did you see him?"

"He said to tell you he's not here. He looks like shit and smells worse. I think he's drunk."

"Bloody hell. The last thing I need is a brother in crisis right now."

After washing the dishes from dinner, Mary Ellen sat on the dock listening to the loons wail in the distance. Her mother sat on the porch, finishing off a bottle of wine. Paula disappeared into the cabin, wearing her iPod earphones, carrying her stack of *Glitter* and *Seventeen* magazines. Mary Ellen tossed a rock into the water. It was going to be a longer-than-long long weekend.

| Mary Ellen woke up to the sound of a slamming door and found her mother rummaging through a kitchen cupboard.

"You're making a lot of noise, Mom."

"My first-aid kit has to be in here somewhere. I took Keith some muffins for breakfast. When I got there, he was sitting on the dock with blood gushing from his hand. Nearly cut his thumb off trying to fix his boat. He should go to the hospital, but he won't. Typical."

Finally, she pulled a box from the cupboard. "I hope I still have some suture thread in here. Aha. Let's go. I might need your help."

"Take Paula."

"She's still in bed. As usual. Besides, Keith likes you."

"Yippee. What about what I like?"

| Mrs. Merriweather showed up at dinnertime. Each summer she looked shorter and rounder. Like a garden gnome. Karen poured wine into two plastic glasses and carried the bottle outside. Soon Mary Ellen and Paula joined the two women at the picnic bench, where they all watched Karen burn the burgers to a black death on the barbecue. Karen swore under her breath as she attempted to flip them. Mary Ellen missed her dad's burgers.

Trigger bounded out of the trees. Paula recoiled when the dog licked her hand.

"Ew. Get away from me, you disgusting mutt. Who brought you here?"

"I did," said Keith, emerging from the lakeside path. He held up his hand. The bloody bandages were shredded. "I tried to chop some wood."

"Jesus, Keith," said Karen. "I told you not to do anything with that hand today. You tore your stitches open."

"Nice to see you, Keith," said Mrs. Merriweather. "You're looking...well, like you need a good meal."

Ten minutes later, a fresh bandage wrapped around his hand, Keith sat down beside Mary Ellen. She smelled whiskey on his breath, but the body odour was gone. At least he knew how to take a shower.

Karen refilled her wine glass. Keith pulled a flask from his back pocket, took a swig, and helped himself to a burger. They watched him chew and finally swallow.

"Christ. If you have any of these left over, Karen, we could use them for hockey pucks."

"Smart ass. They're better than anything you'd cook for yourself. By the way, did you get your invitation to the high-school reunion?"

"I don't read my mail."

"It's next weekend."

"You going?"

"Maybe. You?"

"Not a chance."

"Come on. Don't you want to see how all those girls look twenty years later? Tell us your secret fantasies. Which one were you hot for?"

"Knock it off, Karen."

"I know. One of those bouncy cheerleaders."

Keith glared at his sister.

"Nope. Not your type? Maybe you had a hankering for a brainiac with boobs."

"This sunset is one of the best I've seen," said Mrs. Merriweather. "Look at the oranges and purples in those clouds."

"Sunsets are boring," said Paula.

"Don't be rude, Paula," said Karen.

"That's all right, dear. Perhaps sunsets are boring. But I don't know how many more I'll see."

"What's it like, being old?" said Karen.

"Who said I was old?"

"I'm so sorry, Mrs. M. It must be the wine talking. I didn't mean *old* old, it's just that you're, well, getting old. Old-er. You know, old-ish."

Mrs. Merriweather pushed her plate away and stood up. "I've had enough. Thank you for dinner."

"I'm off too," said Keith, standing up. "I'm going fishing in the morning if anyone wants to join me."

"Fishing?" said Karen. "By yourself? With that hand? No way."

"Come with me then. We used to fish together all the time."

"Yes," said Mrs. Merriweather. "I remember watching both of you and Kerrie-Lynn bob around out there in all kinds of weather."

Mary Ellen and Paula exchanged puzzled looks. "Who's Kerrie-Lynn?"

"Their sister, of course," said Mrs. Merriweather. "Keith's twin. The dead one. The beautiful dead one."

Keith let out a low whistle. Karen stared down at her hands.

"How come we don't know about her?" said Paula.

"She died," said Keith. "Nineteen years ago. Before you were born. Come on, Trigger. Let's go."

Man and dog disappeared into the woods. Karen didn't move. Mary Ellen studied her mother for a few moments before she spoke. "What happened to your sister?"

"She got sick. End of story."

With that, Karen started stacking dishes. Mary Ellen was astonished to see her mother give Mrs. Merriweather an angry look.

The old lady shrugged. "Secrets aren't good for families."

| Keith and Mary Ellen sat in the boat the next morning, each with a fishing rod in hand. Trigger sprawled in the bow. The air was fresh and the water calm under a clear sky. A few birds floated by overhead.

"Sure was surprised to see you show up."

"I was awake. This is better than listening to Mom snore in the next room. And Paula farts when she sleeps. She's such a slug."

"Don't let her get in your wheelhouse. Besides, someday you might like her."

"No way."

"One day she might not be there, and you'll wish she was."

"What was Kerrie-Lynn like?"

"Nice."

"Nice? That's all?"

"Yeah. That's all. She was nice. A hell of a lot nicer than me."

"Nicer than my mother?"

"Your mother's nice, kid. She's been through a lot. And you should be nice to her."

"How did Kerrie-Lynn die?"

"I don't talk about that."

"Why not?"

Mary Ellen saw his lips press harder together. He fiddled with his reel. Then his line went taut and his grip tightened on the rod. "We got ourselves a big one. But I'll break my stitches again if I try to land it myself."

He shoved the rod at Mary Ellen. The fish tugged hard and almost pulled it out of her hands.

"I can't do this."

"Sure you can. I'll talk you through."

A few minutes later, Keith placed a glistening walleye in Mary Ellen's arms. "About fifteen pounds. A good size. Nice work."

Mary Ellen liked the way the fish's eye reflected the sky. Keith watched her gaze at her catch. "It's up to you, kid. Does the fish live or die?"

"It lives."

Keith lowered the fish back into the lake. They watched it swim away. A moment later, a bald eagle swooped down to the water's surface, not twenty feet from their boat. It plucked a lake trout from the water and soared up again, the fish firmly hooked below, one talon already tearing at the fish's flesh.

"A great touch-and-go," said Keith. "Right on target. That fish didn't have a chance."

"You're back!" Mary Ellen shouted up to the birds, then turned to her uncle.

"Do you think they're same eagles as last year?"

"Could be. They winter down around Arkansas and fly back up here in March. Mate for life. Meet in the air, tumble and tussle on the wing. Now that's something to see. The bigger one is the female."

They turned their attention back to their rods. Off the front of the boat, a huge walleye leaped out of the water. Mary Ellen felt the splash on her arm. "Wow. That one was bigger than mine."

"You can fish with me anytime this summer, kid. You're good luck."

"Okay, but I'm not going to stop asking questions."

Back at the dock, Mary Ellen carried the tackle box up to the deck. Keith leaned the fishing rods against the railing, then turned to his niece.

"You're a lot like her, kid. Kerrie-Lynn let most of her fish go, too. And she loved those eagles."

| That night, after Karen fell asleep on the couch, Mary Ellen poured the splash of wine left in her mother's bottle down the sink. She and Paula cleaned up the cabin and packed for the morning's trip back to the city. Before heading to their beds, Mary Ellen threw a blanket over Karen, and Paula turned out the lights.

The Smart Sisters

MELANIE SMART CONTEMPLATED her only remaining asset. Her eyes lingered on each component: the shiny cymbals, saucy tom-toms, snappy snare, proud hi-hat, the commanding copper bass. Her sigh bounced around the empty room, off the peeling walls, and dusty chandelier. She dreaded what she had to do that night, didn't know how she would force herself to sell her drums back to the guy she bought them from, way back when she first came to Paris, eight years ago now.

The doorbell made her jump. Hoping it wasn't the landlord again, she cracked the door open for a one-eyed peek. A young man stood on the step.

"Oui?"

"Melanie Smart?"

She nodded, letting the door fall wide open.

"Signez ici," he said, thrusting out a clipboard.

"Pourquoi?"

"Merde!" He looked at the sky. "L'envoyé par coursier, Madame. Signez."

Since when had she gone from Mademoiselle to Madame? Melanie scrawled an illegible version of her name and took the slim package. It felt foreign in her hand. Melanie stepped outside and watched the truck disappear down the street before looking down at the envelope. She rarely received mail, much less a courier package. Sinking down onto her front steps, she scanned the label for the sender's name. *Earl Stanfield? Crap. This can't be good.*

A plump grey pigeon fluttered down from a nearby roof to join its friends on the ground, pecking at scraps of bread scattered in front of the crumbling steps. Melanie's stoop was unremarkable, one in a row of identical seedy porches on a short, narrow thoroughfare filled with human and vehicle noise. At one end of the street, a series of cafés led to the promise of a Paris boulevard. At the other, the building facades grew shabbier and shabbier. Off in the distance, the ivory silhouette of Sacré Coeur's basilica shimmered over Montmartre as if suspended from the sky.

Melanie opened the envelope, pulled out a two-page letter, and read the last page first. It outlined a travel itinerary that included a limo ride to the airport, a one-way ticket back to Canada on a flight leaving Orly the next day, with another limo ride waiting when she landed. She flipped to the cover letter, scanned it once, then read it again, more slowly this time. Fuzzy images fluttered through her head: a sweeping staircase, a red Corvette at the bottom of a lake, a grey fedora on a church pew. *He's dead? He can't be dead.* She could still hear his flat baritone voice in her head, growling out the last words she'd heard him say.

"Run off then. I'll have Earl write you a cheque for five thousand dollars. You'll be back as soon as it's gone. I give you a month, two at the most."

A blob of pigeon shit landed on Melanie's bare foot. She scraped it off on the step and stood up. The white "Declaration d'eviction" notice stapled to the door gleamed in the sunlight. In the window beside the door, she caught her reflection, dark brown hair dishevelled, face wan. She looked too tired to be only twenty-seven. A flash of herself at age three crossed her mind. She tried to pull up her parents' faces but couldn't, only an image of her own small toddler hand held in a larger one. Melanie saw this vision often. Whenever it entered her mind, she scolded her little girl self: *Look up, you idiot, look up.*

Melanie sat down at her drums, picked up her sticks, and launched into her version of "Wipeout." She'd been practicing this one for weeks, but hadn't once nailed it. Until today. Now the rolls and cymbal crashes flowed out again and again. She worked the moves into her muscle memory until her armpits streamed sweat. Her eyes turned once more to the letter lying on the floor. *Hmm. First class. That could be fun.* And maybe she wouldn't have to pay for extra luggage.

As she began to pack, she wondered how her sisters were reacting to this news. Her sisters. It was about time she saw them again.

| Abigail Smart and her two sons came out of the unemployment office and wandered down the steps. The area was crowded, even at seven in the morning. The late October air was warmer than usual. Those who hadn't arrived early enough to land a job for the day loitered on the sidewalk. Some slouched against the building, smoking. A few dozed on a nearby grassy patch. Others sat staring into space. Most were men.

Abby looked at her watch. Another hour before she could drop the boys off at school. She felt a rising wave of panic and swallowed to quell it. What did her parents used to say? Their voices were fading as she got older, but if she focused, she could still hear them. *Keep calm*, from her mother. *You can do it*, from her father.

"I'm hungry," said Andrew.

"Me too," said Adam. "Can we get something to eat?"

Abby sighed. She reached into her purse for her wallet and pulled a twenty from the secret flap, the place she kept cash in case of an emergency. With the twenty gone, her stash was empty.

"Sure. Why not? Let's celebrate something, anything."

They started down the block. A black sedan with tinted windows pulled up beside them. Abby didn't notice until the vehicle slowed to their walking pace. Suddenly on alert, she quickened their steps and put herself between the boys and the car, but it stopped in front of them at the next intersection. A man wearing dark sunglasses emerged. His face had no expression and his shoulders were wide. He looked like a robot wearing a suit.

"Abigail Smart?" He loomed over her.

She pulled the boys closer. "Who wants to know?"

Robot-man took an envelope from his pocket. "A delivery from Mr. Stanfield."

Hearing that name made Abby smooth her skirt and stand up straighter as she opened the envelope. It contained a short letter: *I regret to inform you*. . .Abby's hand flew to her mouth as a small gasp escaped.

"I am instructed to collect you and your sons tomorrow morning at nine o'clock," said Robot-man.

She nodded. "We live at. . ."

"I know where you live."

Abby stared at the letter in her hand. Unlike her parents' voices, her grandfather's was still fresh in her mind. His words from that last night felt etched on her skin.

"I don't know why I'm surprised, Abigail. You might be a teacher, but you're not brainy. Breeding is your only talent. Let's hope it's a boy. I don't need another girl in this family. Try for a husband next time. Until then, see Earl for funds."

Abby and the boys watched the car disappear down the street.

"That guy was weird," said Adam.

"What's wrong, Mom?" said Andrew.

"My grandfather is dead."

The boys gave each other puzzled looks, then turned back to their mother. Their words came out in unison.

"You have a grandfather?"

| In a small strip mall, a shoe store was in the dying throes of its final sale. Big red signs filled the window: "CLOSING FOREVER. EVERYTHING MUST GO." Inside, customers lined up at the cash desk, each one balancing several boxes. Two harried cashiers struggled to process the sales. Behind them, standing near a small office at the back of the store—an office that used to be hers—Sara Smart watched the clamour, a bundle of manila file folders in her arms. A tall trim woman in her mid-thirties, she wore a plain tailored suit, her fair hair pulled back into a ponytail.

"Now they come," she said under her breath as she surveyed the shop's sudden wealth of customers, the flurry of activity in her usually empty store.

An accountant emerged from the office behind her.

"These are the last of them," said Sara as she handed him the files. The accountant watched her for a moment, a hint of sympathy in his eyes.

"There's no need for you to be here. The bank will do the rest."

"Thanks, but I'll stay."

"Suit yourself." He vanished back into the office.

Sara wandered around the shop, finding mates for discarded shoes. She was kneeling on the floor gathering boxes when the black sedan pulled up and parked outside. The driver entered the store and walked directly over to her.

"Sara Smart?"

She saw his feet and didn't bother to look up. " There's nothing left, so go away."

He held an envelope in the air. " You need to read this."

Sara stood up and studied him. "Do I know you?"

He waved the envelope close to her face. She took it, opened the letter, and scanned the page. Then she crumpled it up, and threw it on the floor. "So he's dead. I couldn't care less."

"Mr. Stanfield said to tell you that your presence tomorrow is imperative. I will pick you up at nine in the morning."

" Tell Mr. Stanfield I'll show up on my own. I don't need your ride."

| In the early moments of its daily arc across the sky, the late October sun offered little warmth. Leafless trees, their bare branches open to the burnished light, created stark frames for the walk-up apartment buildings on the street where Abby and her boys lived.

The black sedan soon left the city behind. On both sides of the highway, the countryside stretched out flat and brown, the land shorn of its crops, ready for winter's blanket. The sedan maintained a steady moderate speed, staying behind an ageing green Mustang convertible. After two hours, the small convoy turned onto a smaller road, passing a large sign: "WELCOME TO PEREGRINE LAKE. PLEASE DRIVE COURTEOUSLY."

Sara guided the Mustang down the main street, keeping her eyes fixed on the road, not wanting to see whether or not her old hometown looked the same as it had eight years ago. At the cemetery gates, she turned, steered the car up the short driveway, and stopped in front of a small chapel. The sedan pulled in behind her.

The driver opened the door for Abby and the boys. They emerged and waited. Sara sat for a long moment before getting out of her car.

"Hello Sara," said Abby.

"Abby," said Sara, with a slight nod.

Abby nudged the boys, who responded dutifully in unison. "Hello, Aunt Sara."

"Why are the boys here? This is no place for children."

"Where I go, they go. They're part of the family."

"Lucky them."

The driver pointed them away from the chapel, across the driveway to a courtyard surrounded by limestone walls filled with rows of small vaults. A cool wind gusted from behind, blowing dried brown leaves past their feet.

In the courtyard, a gold urn sat on a pedestal covered with a white cloth. One door in the vault wall was open, the small cavern yawning empty. Next to the urn stood a man in his early sixties, wearing an immaculate suit and matching fedora. His face was weathered but handsome, the kind of face an unknown actor playing a friendly manager in a bank commercial might have. His posture was that of someone who has handled many difficult situations with aplomb.

"Welcome ladies," he said. "And young men."

"Thank you for the ride, Mr. Stanfield," said Abby.

"My pleasure, Abigail."

Sara pointed to the urn. "Is that him?"

He nodded. "And hello to you too, Sara."

"Can we just get on with it?"

"We will wait for the rest of the family. The other car is almost here."

Several long silent minutes passed before another black sedan appeared through the gates. The trunk was half-open, its lid strapped down with bungee cords securing a variety of odd-shaped cases.

Melanie unfolded her long legs from the back seat and stretched her arms up over her head. She moved into a few body twists to work out her traveller's kinks. Clad in clunky black army boots, torn blue jeans, and an orange poncho, the youngest Smart sister had a large silver cross hanging from a black leather thong draped around her neck.

"Melanie!" said Abby. Melanie accepted Abby's hug, but did not return it.

Abby pulled back. "It's so good to see you, Mel."

"You too. These must be my nephews."

Adam and Andrew stared at the new arrival. Abby shushed them when they pointed at her boots and began to laugh. Melanie did a quick one-two stomp, and winked at the boys.

"Thanks for the plane ticket, Mr. Stanfield. How did you find me?"

"We have always known where to find you, my dear. Welcome home."

Melanie moved to the pedestal and bent down close to the urn. "How are you doing in there, Gramps? Hope you're not claustrophobic."

She turned to Sara, who stood motionless off to one side. "Hey, big sis."

"That's quite the outfit, Mel. Very appropriate." Sara pointed to the cross. "When did you get religion?"

Melanie tugged at the heavy piece of silver. "Snagged it at a flea market."

"She's weird," whispered Adam to his mother. Abby shushed him.

"Now that we're all here, we can move your grandfather to his final resting place."

"Shouldn't we have a funeral?" said Melanie.

"Jacob requested that we hold no service of any kind."

"No service? Is that proper?" said Abby.

"Fine with me," said Sara.

Mr. Stanfield gestured to the urn and the open vault door. "Who wants to do the honours?"

All three sisters took a step backward. The boys rushed forward.

"I will, I will," said Andrew, reaching for the urn.

"I'm eight. You're only six," said Adam, getting to the urn before his brother.

"Please don't fight, boys," said Abby.

"Can I look inside?" said Adam.

Mr. Stanfield took the urn away from Adam and put it in the vault. The door sealed with a loud click.

"Shouldn't we say something?" said Abby.

"How about this? I'm glad the old bastard is dead," said Sara.

"I meant a eulogy or a prayer."

"All right, then. Thank God he's dead. Amen."

Adam and Andrew giggled. Abby silenced them with a look.

"I urge you all to remember that it was your grandfather who took you in after your parents' tragic accident."

Mr. Stanfield's comment evoked only stony silence. The three sisters stood with their arms crossed as they glared at the man in the suit. He pointed toward the vehicles.

"I think we're done here. I've arranged for you to have lunch before the reading of Jacob's will."

" The will? Already?" said Abby.

" Where?" said Sara.

"At the house, of course."

"Can't we go someplace else? Your office, or a restaurant, or something?"

"Unfortunately, no. Jacob's instructions were quite clear. We will meet at the house. Enjoy your lunch. I'll join you afterwards."

He strolled to a car waiting at the main gate. Sara, Abby, and the boys moved in the direction of their cars. As they crossed the driveway, Sara couldn't stop herself from glancing up the road that wound through the cemetery, up to where their parents lay, side by side, cold and still for almost two decades now.

Behind them, Melanie hadn't moved from beside the vault. She looked at the closed door in the wall. A simple inscription was already in place: "JACOB EDWARD SMART—*Peace*." Melanie reached out and touched her fingers to the words, tapping one beat on each of his names, lingering on the last word.

"Goodbye, Gramps," she said, and ran to catch up with her sisters.

| Peregrine Lake, the body of water, is shallow and wide, so wide that in many places one side of the lake is not easily visible from the other. Peregrine Lake, the town, is small. For three seasons of the year, the town's permanent population hovers around five thousand, all of whom refer to their community as Perry

Pond, some with more affection than others. In the summer, everything changes. The town's population triples as cottage owners from the city return to fill the beaches, restaurants, shops, and arcades until the fall.

Now the streets were quiet as the vehicles progressed along Lakefront Drive. The sedan carrying Abby and the boys led the way, Sara's Mustang following behind. Melanie's car brought up the rear.

Situated outside the town limits, Jacob Smart's lakeside mansion was the oldest and largest structure in the area. The estate consisted of several buildings scattered around four acres of land: a garage, a gatekeeper's cabin, a boathouse, and a guest-house with four separate suites. At the centre of the property was a two-storey main house with a veranda and a corner turret. Access to the turret's roof was via a metal ladder leading up to a viewing platform topped by a weather vane.

The three-vehicle convoy stopped at the main house. The mansion's shutters were askew. Its exterior façade was missing bricks and stones. The spacious veranda was marred by gaps where several planks had rotted away. All the painted surfaces were faded and peeling.

"It looks just the same," said Abby. "Well, sort of the same."

"I remember it looking a lot better than this," said Melanie.

"I try not to remember it at all," said Sara.

Several thuds behind them distracted their attention from the house. They turned to see Melanie's luggage—one shabby suitcase and all the odd-shaped boxes—sitting on the ground. Abby's driver paid Melanie's driver, who immediately drove off. Abby's driver then got into the car they came in and also drove away.

"How are we going to get home, Mom?" said Andrew.

"You can come with me. I'm leaving right now." Sara said as she started toward the Mustang.

A woman emerged from the mansion's front door. She wore an old-style waitress's uniform complete with apron: her hair was a blue-grey helmet, her mouth a wide slash, downturned at the corners. She marched to the top of the steps and stood with her hands on her hips.

"Mrs. Cooper?" said Melanie. "Is that you?"

Andrew hid behind his mother. "Who is that?"

"I see the orphans have returned," said Mrs. Cooper. "And multiplied." She glowered at the boys. Adam moved behind his little brother.

Melanie took a deep breath. "You're looking well, Mrs. Cooper."

"Hah! I look like hell. Don't stand there like a bunch of ninnies. Lunch is in the dining room."

She disappeared back into the house. No one moved until Abby took each of her sons by the hand. "It has been a long time since breakfast. Come on, boys. Let's go eat."

Melanie followed them. Halfway up the steps, she looked back. Sara was still at the bottom, not moving. Melanie went down and pulled her up, none too gently, one riser at a time.

Once inside, the sisters squinted to pierce the gloom. The house was so dark it could have been the middle of the night. Heavy curtains shrouded the windows. Peering into the roomy parlour off the foyer, the girls saw dingy white sheets covering the furniture. The soaring staircase rose into blackness. At the top, a ring of light illuminated a life-sized portrait of Jacob Smart. He seemed to peer down at them, looking right through them. The girls turned away.

Mrs. Cooper appeared beside the stairs.

"Well? Are you going to eat or not?"

She opened the doors to the dining room and tapped her foot, waiting for them to enter.

Unlike the parlour, the dining room was filled with light. Its furniture gleamed. The mahogany table was set for five. On the sideboard by the window was a steaming soup tureen, a selection of sandwiches, a tray of pickles, and a fruit platter. A large silver punch bowl held pop and juices on ice. Coffee aromas wafted from a carafe sitting on a hot plate.

"What, no wine?" said Melanie.

Mrs. Cooper closed the door behind her.

| The sisters picked at their lunches. Adam and Andrew ate everything they could. When their appetites were satisfied, the boys started throwing buns at each other. Then pickles. One landed in Sara's lap. Sara frowned at Andrew. In return, he crossed his eyes at her.

She took a handful of his shirt and pulled him to within inches of her face. "Your eyes will get stuck that way, and you'll look stupid for the rest of your life."

"Will not."

"He already looks stupid," said Adam.

"Do not."

"Do so."

Andrew wrenched himself from Sara's grasp and hit Adam. Adam hit back and they fell to the floor. Abby heaved a sigh as she watched them wrestle. "Boys, please don't fight." She tossed a despairing look at her sister. "Now look what you've done."

"Me?" said Sara. "They're your kids. I'm only the benevolent aunt."

The boys rolled into a plant stand holding a potted fig tree. It crashed to the floor. Melanie and Abby pulled the wrestlers apart. Abby restrained Adam, while Melanie grappled with Andrew. Sara toyed with her sandwich as if she were alone in the room.

Adam escaped his mother's grasp and dove under the table. Abby dove after him. Melanie pinned Andrew on the floor. He struggled, but couldn't escape.

"You're mean! Just like her," said Andrew, looking from Melanie to Sara.

"Charming," said Sara. "Abby, do you practice any parental discipline at all?"

Abby finally managed to pull Adam from under the table. "That's enough. You two go outside. There's a big yard to explore. Just don't go outside the front gate."

The boys ran off, laughing as they raced each other to the door.

"And stay away from the lake!"

"I like your boys," said Melanie, after a few moments of awkward silence.

"Thanks. I'm lucky. They're good kids."

"Hah! They're hellions," said Sara. "You have to get tougher with them, Abby."

"I disagree. Children need a gentle touch. Especially when they have only one parent. You don't know how hard it is to raise kids alone."

"That'll teach you to sleep with every guy who comes knocking on your door."

"That's bitchy," said Melanie. "Even for you, Sara."

"I'd rather be a bitch than a coward. At least I don't run away when things get tough."

"I didn't run away," said Melanie. "I went elsewhere."

"Are you saying that your sudden departure had nothing to do with the fact that your boyfriend impregnated your sister?" said Sara.

Abby looked as if she'd been punched. "It wasn't like that. I never meant to..."

Sara leaned closer to Melanie. "You'll be happy to know he didn't stick around long after you took off. Neither did the next one. They never do."

"You are a miserable witch, Sara," said Melanie. "The only thing missing is a hairy wart on your chin."

Mrs. Cooper appeared in the doorway. "Finished eating?"

Silence fell as the housekeeper gathered up the dishes. The sisters made no move to help until one plate teetered on the edge of the pile. Abby caught it before it fell.

"Mrs. Cooper, why is the house all closed up?" said Melanie. "Gramps has only been dead for three days."

"Jacob didn't use much of the house. Here, his office, and his bedroom. Other than the kitchen, the rest of the place has been shut down for years. You'd know that if you'd ever bothered to come home."

After Mrs. Cooper left, silence fell once more. Abby leaned against the window, keeping an eye on the boys in the yard. Melanie's hands ran through drumming patterns on the tabletop, oblivious to Sara's irritated glances. Somewhere in the house, a clock chimed.

Sara stood up and walked from one end of the room to the other. She checked her watch. "I wonder what time Mr. Stanfield will grace us with his presence?"

"How much do you think Gramps was worth?" said Melanie.

Abby shrugged. "No idea."

"More than a million for sure," said Sara. "Maybe three."

"I guess I should have sent him a Christmas card. At least you were both close enough to visit once in a while."

An uncomfortable look passed between Sara and Abby.

"You did visit, didn't you?"

They didn't answer.

"Okay. How long has it been since you saw him?"

Her sisters looked down at their hands.

"A year?...Two?...Five? Sara?" asked Abby.

Sara looked up at the ceiling and shook her head.

Melanie threw up her arms. "For Christ's sake..."

"Eight," said Sara.

"Yes, eight," said Abby.

"Eight years? Both of you? Not since I left?"

Sara and Abby nodded.

"Well, that cuts us out of the will. What do you think it says?"

"Probably another lecture," said Sara. "I can hear it now: *You owe it to your father's memory to make something of yourself, young lady.*"

"Not exactly," said a voice from the door. "Shall we move to Jacob's office?"

| Earl Stanfield sat in the wingback chair behind Jacob's desk. Bookshelves filled one wall. Anonymous ancestors stared down from various oil paintings. Above the credenza behind the desk was another portrait of Jacob.

"Mrs. Cooper will keep an eye on the children while we chat. Have a seat, ladies."

Sara, Abby, and Melanie sat on three stiff chairs placed in front of the desk. Mr. Stanfield began reading and didn't look up until he'd finished reciting the will's contents.

"...signed and dated the thirty-first day of December, last year."

When the sisters eventually found their voices, the words came out in a simultaneous stream.

"Thirty million dollars?"

"What does all that mean?"

"You've got to be kidding."

"There is no kidding in a will," said the lawyer.

Sara covered her face with her hands. "I won't do it."

"You have that choice."

"I'm not sure I understand," said Abby. "We have to live together? Here?"

Melanie jumped to her feet. "How did Gramps get thirty million dollars?"

Sara leaned over the desk. "Did you put him up to this?"

"One question at a time, please." Mr. Stanfield stood up behind the desk. "Your grandfather was an astute man. As you know, he owned three successful auto dealerships. His other investments, real estate and the like, have done well. Jacob managed his assets wisely."

Abby rubbed her forehead. "I must have missed something. We have to live here? In this house? Together? Why?"

Sara pounded her fist on the desk. "He can't do this."

"Yes, he can. While unusual, this will meets normal standards."

Melanie let out a low whistle. "Ten million each. Unbelievable."

"You didn't answer me," said Sara. "This was your idea, right?"

"On the contrary. I advised Jacob against this. The will was entirely his doing. My job now is to ensure that his last wishes are carried out."

The lawyer watched the sisters' astonished faces for a few moments. Then he sat down again. "Let me help you by going over it one more time. Listen carefully."

"I loathe him."

"Jeez, Sara," said Melanie. "He just left us a pisspot full of money. And still you 'loathe' him?"

"Ladies. Are you going to listen or not?"

Three mouths closed as their faces turned back to him.

"I will summarize the will as clearly as I can. Jacob's estate is to be divided equally between the three of you, AFTER you have fulfilled two conditions. First, you must live together in this house for a period of one year."

He paused to make eye contact with each sister. "Is that understood?"

Melanie nodded. Abby nodded. Sara frowned.

"Good. Next, the three of you will be given a total of $100,000 today. At the end of one year, you must still have $100,000. Do you understand?"

"That's the part I don't get."

"What part don't you 'get', Abigail?"

"How are we going to live if we can't spend any of the money?"

"That's for you three to figure out. Jobs might help, perhaps an entrepreneurial project or two. You do not have to have the same $100,000 at the end of the year, merely a bank account with an unencumbered balance of $100,000."

The sisters began talking all at once. Mr. Stanfield held up his hands to silence them.

"In conclusion, if you do not fulfill these two conditions, the entire estate will be donated to a charity trust for the local theatre company."

"That's impossible," said Sara. "Grandfather thought stage plays were a ridiculous waste of time. He once told me that he hoped that damned theatre would go bankrupt. Why would he leave them all his money?"

Mr. Stanfield ignored her and continued his summary. "If you accept the first condition, but fall short of meeting the second condition after one year, the initial $100,000, which you will obviously no longer have, is yours. If you choose not to accept the conditions of the will, you will receive the $100,000 right now, split evenly among the three of you."

He looked up, from one sister to the next to the next, meeting their surly scrutiny without flinching.

"I won't stay here."

"That's your choice, Sara. That violates the first condition. I will have three cheques for $33,333.67 issued immediately."

Melanie looked at her sisters, but neither one would look back at her. She moved around behind their chairs and knelt between the two of them.

"Let's not be hasty. We should think about this."

"I have a headache. I can't think."

"Take an aspirin, Abby. We need to talk."

"Not here," said Sara.

Melanie turned back to the man behind the desk.

"Earl...may we call you Earl? And would you excuse us for a few minutes?"

"Yes to both questions. By all means. Get some fresh air. Go for a walk together. I can wait. You have one hour."

The sisters filed out of the office. Earl stood up, muttering to himself. "Jacob, what have you done?"

| Sara burst out of the mansion's front door and took the porch stairs two at a time, Melanie and Abby running to keep up with her. She started for the Mustang, but Abby took her sister's arm and pulled her in the direction Melanie had taken, toward the lake.

"It's just a conversation, Sara. It can't hurt to talk," said Abby.

Sara snatched her arm away from Abby's grasp, but followed her sisters. Abby waved to Adam and Andrew, who were climbing a tree near the garage, with Mrs. Cooper watching from a lawn chair nearby.

Near the boathouse, Sara and Abby sank down onto a log beside a firepit. Abby looked around. The grounds of the estate were wild, overgrown. The soaring hollyhocks that once created a border lay sprawled on the ground in a brown snarled mess. Perennials and weeds tangled together in the flowerbeds. The angel statue in the middle of the empty pond was missing a wing. Abby spread her arms out in dismay.

"It used to be so pretty back here. What happened to the garden? And look at the croquet lawn. It's full of weeds."

Melanie squatted down in front of her sisters, picked up a dead twig, and snapped it into three equal pieces.

"Let me get this straight, Sara. You're ready to walk away from ten million dollars. EACH."

She held the three twig pieces up one at a time. " That's ten for you, ten for Abby, ten for…"

"I don't want anything from him."

"Neither do I," said Abby.

Sara tossed a stone into the bushes. "Don't you see? He's controlling us from the grave."

Melanie pointed one of the twigs at her oldest sister. "He's dead. He can't control us anymore, Sara. All we have to do is satisfy the conditions of the will."

"I don't think I want the money, Mel," said Abby. "It's such a lot. Let's split the hundred grand. Thirty thousand dollars will set me and the boys up just fine."

"That's peanuts. It'll be gone in six months. You have an opportunity to give your boys much more than that."

"But they just started at a new school. It's hard on children to change schools."

"I can give you ten million reasons why they'll get over it."

Abby rubbed her hands on her arms, and Sara straightened herself on the log.

"How can you squat like that for so long, Mel? I can't do that. Can you, Sara?"

Melanie's squat tilted closer to her sisters.

"All right. I'll level with you. I haven't had a gig in three months. I've been evicted from my apartment. When I got that letter, I was ready to pawn my drums. I could use a quick thirty grand. Hell, I'd be out of here on the first plane to anywhere. But ten million dollars? That's a lifetime of freedom, and I'm not walking away from it."

Melanie looked from Abby to Sara, and back to Abby again. "What are you doing with your life right now? Are you teaching?"

Abby hesitated before answering. "No. I was a substitute last year. I'd hoped for a permanent position this year, but the education budget has been cut again. Right now I'm...looking for a job."

Melanie turned to Sara. "And you? That cozy little bookstore must be making you rich."

Sara met Melanie's gaze but said nothing.

"Shoe store," said Abby. "Sara bought a shoe store after the coffee shop went under."

Melanie raised her eyebrows. Sara scowled at Abby, who continued, oblivious to her older sister's discomfort: "The bookstore was forced out of business four years ago when a big national chain went in down the street."

Sara's look grew harder with each word. Still Abby went on. "After that, Sara bought the cutest little coffee shop. I liked it so much. They made the best cappuccinos, but it lasted only a year because two new coffee shops opened up in the same block, so then she bought the..."

"Thank you so much for that recap of my business affairs, Abby. Are you sure you didn't forget anything?"

Melanie stood up and slapped her thigh with her hand. "I don't believe it. Perfect Sara blew it. Twice."

Sara took a deep breath. "Three times. The bank took over the shoe store last week."

Abby gasped. "That's why I haven't seen you for so long. Why didn't you call me? Why don't you ever tell me anything?"

"So. You're as broke as we are, Sara," said Melanie. "And yet you can't stand the thought of spending a year with your sisters so we can each claim ten million."

"It's not us together so much. It's that house. Nothing but sadness in there."

"So what? We've lived here before. We can do it again for a while. It's huge. We'll never have to see each other."

"And what about the money?" said Sara. "Clearly, none of us are financial geniuses. How are we going to have $100,000 left at the end of the year? We'll end up right back where we are now."

"That's not going to happen. Maybe we'll auction off some of those gloomy old paintings to the cottage people. Or we'll go into town and get nothing jobs. It's only a year. We'll put our heads together and figure something out. After all, we are the smart sisters."

Melanie looked for a reaction to their old rallying cry, the words Sara used to whisper to the younger girls when they woke up afraid in the night, something that happened often in the years after their parents died: "*Come on, we can get through this. WE are the smart sisters.*"

The three sat in silence for several minutes.

"All right," said Abby. "I'm in. But you both have to be nice to my boys."

Melanie and Abby stood together. They turned to Sara, who looked out at the lake. After a moment, she nodded her head.

The three moved forward to hug each other. When the clumsy embrace ended, Melanie punched the air. "You'll see. It'll be easy. Morceau de gâteau."

Abby and Sara looked confused.

"Seriously? No boarding-school French left in your heads? Let's go find Earl."

| Earl stood behind the desk, keys in hand. "A wise decision, ladies."

Melanie reached for the keys, but Earl held them back.

"First, some ground rules. Mrs. Cooper resides in the gate-keeper's cabin. It's off limits. Jacob provided for her to stay there as long as she lives. She's no longer the housekeeper."

"And the hundred grand?"

"A joint account has been set up at the local bank. See the manager as soon as you're settled."

Melanie again held her hand out for the keys, but Earl continued with his instructions.

"Estate funds will take care of basic costs such as electricity, heat, and so on. But you are responsible for all your personal expenses."

The sisters nodded, but Earl still wasn't finished. "Under no circumstances are you to sell anything from the estate. It does not belong to you."

"Yet," said Melanie, holding out her hand.

Earl continued. "Sara and Abigail's personal effects will be delivered this evening. Be aware that I am obligated to check on you at random intervals throughout the year."

"Sure," said Abby. "Just let us know when you're coming."

"That would hardly be random. You can expect me to pop in at any time."

The sisters followed Earl down the hall to the foyer, where he handed the keys to Sara. Melanie accompanied him out onto the veranda. "Can I ask you a question?"

"By all means."

"Who wrote the inscription on Gramps' vault?"

"Jacob wrote it himself. I simply followed his instructions."

"The word 'Peace' doesn't sound like him."

"You'd be surprised at how often he used it in the last few years. I wish you the best of luck."

After a courtly bow, Earl walked down the steps. Melanie stepped inside. Moments later, she was back out with another question for Earl, but he was gone. Vanished. She walked the length of the veranda and looked in all directions. No sign of him. She shook her head. "Magic man. Here one minute, gone the next."

Melanie rejoined her sisters inside. Perhaps to avoid looking at each other, they all turned their faces up to the ceiling, where the candelabra chandelier seemed to sway. Once more, their eyes went to their grandfather's portrait at the top of the stairs. Was that a slight smile on his face? Squeaks, scratches, and muted scurrying sounds came from behind walls. The late afternoon sun was now low in the sky. Shadows grew in every corner.

"Yikes! The boys! I have to find the boys," said Abby, running out the door.

In the parlour, Melanie pulled sheets from the furniture. Dust clouds blossomed and a mouse raced across the floor.

Sara sat on the veranda steps, watching Abby break the news to the boys. Beyond them, at a window in the gatekeeper's cabin, a curtain drew back and fell into place a few seconds later.

That evening, a solemn group of five sat in the dining room, empty pizza boxes scattered across the table. Their faces were now as tired as they were glum.

"Cheer up, everybody," said Melanie. "This will be fun. Think of it as an adventure."

"Come on boys," said Abby. "Let's check out my old room upstairs. We'll bunk in together for tonight."

In the foyer, three separate piles of luggage had appeared at the bottom of the staircase.

"Creepy," said Sara. "To think that robotic stranger went through my stuff and packed for me."

"He does look like a robot," said Melanie.

"Robot-man. I'd like to take his pulse. See if he has a heart," said Abby, handing one suitcase to each of the boys and picking up her own. Side by side, they climbed the wide stairs.

Sara and Melanie wandered outside and stood on the veranda. The evening was warm for this time of year.

"Look. A shooting star."

"I wish I was on it," said Sara as she went back inside.

"Me too," said Melanie to the air. "Me too."

For a while, she marched back and forth, using the entire length of the veranda, pounding out an air drum solo as she went. Eventually, she stopped at the old swing chair, built for two. Using her poncho to thrash dust off the cushion, she sat down gingerly, testing the strength of the old seat. Then she let herself fall back and threw the poncho over her body. Across the yard, a light in the gatekeeper's cabin went dark.

| A cool frosty morning followed that first night. After foraging through the kitchen, Sara managed to find a can of coffee grounds and a coffeemaker. Her search revealed this to be the full extent of their food supplies. Any hint of what went into making yesterday's lunch had vanished, along with the leftovers. The refrigerator was completely empty, the cupboards and the pantry equally so.

Wrapped in heavy sweaters, Sara and Melanie sat at the kitchen table, their hands around steaming mugs of weak coffee.

"Where'd you sleep?" asked Melanie.

"On a couch in the parlour. You?"

"I fell asleep on the porch and woke up freezing a few hours later. Stumbled up the stairs to my old room. Other than a layer of dust, it hasn't changed."

"I haven't been upstairs yet."

"It's warmer up there than down here," said Melanie.

They sat in silence for a few moments.

"I was sorry to hear about your business…difficulties," said Melanie.

Sara shrugged but said nothing. A few moments later, Melanie broke the silence again.

"Remember when Earl finished reading the will yesterday? He said that Gramps signed it at the end of December last year."

"So?"

"So that's only ten months ago. That means he probably spent last Christmas sitting alone in this house thinking about us. Maybe he'd been thinking about making a new will for a while. Maybe he knew he didn't have much time left."

"He was seventy-five," said Sara. "Nobody who's seventy-five has much time left."

"I suppose. But it's such a strange will. I wonder what was in his head. What do you think the word 'Peace' meant to him? He wasn't exactly a hippie."

"Don't know, don't care," said Sara. She refilled her coffee cup and brought the pot over to top up her sister's as well. As she poured, she sniffed the air. "You're a little ripe, Mel. When was the last time you had a shower?"

"I can't remember, but I know it was on a different continent."

| Sara wandered out the back door toward the lake. To her right was the firepit area where she and her sisters made their deal yesterday. Behind it, the boathouse was shuttered. To her left was the large guesthouse cottage, also shuttered. She went to a window and pulled at one of the panels. It creaked open. Sara peered through the grimy glass. The interior was nothing but dust and darkness, so she couldn't see much. That didn't

matter. Sara remembered it. She also remembered how much her mother had liked it. Janet's voice echoed in her head: "The guesthouse is the best part of that whole place. Your dad and I would meet in there to get away from your grandfather and that nosy Mrs. Cooper."

The guesthouse was also where Sara and her sisters were that morning, Sara rubbing the sleep out of her eyes as Mrs. Cooper brushed her hair and made her put her robe on over her pajamas. Where she sat on the bed with Abby beside her and Melanie on her lap when their grandfather came into the room. She was expecting her parents, not him. Sara could still picture the moment her parents had left them the day before. Janet turned to wave at them one more time, calling back to her oldest daughter: "See you in the morning, sunshine. Look after your little sisters."

Sara walked from the guesthouse to the dock, where she hunkered down at the lake end. Yes, she could squat like Mel. She balanced her elbows on her knees and her chin in her hands. She held herself like this for as long as she could, teetered, then dropped her butt onto the wood and dangled her feet over the water. The lake looked cold, but it was calm and smelled of algae. In the distance, she heard a train crossing the trestle south of town. At least a mile away, it sounded as if it were rumbling by right next to her. She'd forgotten how clearly sound travels over water.

She lay down, stretching her body over the dock's wooden planks, arms and legs splayed like Da Vinci's *Vitruvian Man*, perfectly still under the umbrella of the overcast sky. Gazing up at the clouds, she felt the presence of the ten-year-old girl she'd been prior to the accident. Over the years, when she allowed herself to think about that part of her life, she'd thought of herself as two distinctly different ten-year-olds: the one before the accident, and the one afterward. Before-the-accident Sara did what girls that age do: went to school, played with her friends, left her room in a mess. Thinking wasn't part of that Sara's life. But after-the-accident Sara couldn't stop thinking.

Sara woke to Andrew's eyes two inches from her face. She lurched upwards and they bonked foreheads. "Ouch!" said Sara, rubbing her brow.

Andrew rubbed his head, too. "Mom says you should come in for something to eat."

Sara roused herself, and aunt and nephew walked back to the house together.

"What did you boys do this morning?" asked Sara.

"Mom and Aunt Mel took us into town. It's small."

"Yes, it is."

"But it has a beach. That's cool."

"It's nice in summer. I used to spend a lot of time there."

"Mom says we have to start school right away."

"Good idea."

"Did you go to school here?"

"Only for the first five years. After that, I went to boarding school."

"That must have been fun. Going someplace else for school, away from your mom."

"My mom wasn't around then."

"I forgot. Sorry."

"That's okay. You weren't around then, either."

When they reached the kitchen, Abby was preparing lunch.

"I hope you don't mind, Sara. Mel and I borrowed the Mustang so we could get some groceries. There's a new super-market behind the school. I was afraid we'd have to shop at the

Perry Pond General Store for the next year. Mac and cheese is ready on the stove."

"I'm not hungry," said Sara, helping herself to an apple from a bowl on the table. Beside the bowl was a pumpkin, and beside the pumpkin, a pile of candy bags. "What's all this?"

"It's Halloween tomorrow. This gothic old mansion is so creepy, it probably attracts every kid for miles. I'm sure I didn't buy nearly enough candy. And now I have to come up with costumes for the boys. I'd forgotten how big this place is. Six bedrooms! I moved my stuff into the room next to my old one. Andrew and Adam may as well stay in there together. They can keep each other company."

"Do you ever breathe between sentences, Abby?"

Abby took in a huge breath, blew it all at Sara, and continued. "Mel and I figured you could have the big master bedroom with the turret sitting area and all."

"Not a chance. I'd never sleep a wink. I'll be like you and take my old room. Mel can have the big one."

A crash came from above, followed by another, and another. The beginnings of a drum solo.

Sara looked at the ceiling. "Did you happen to pick up any earplugs while you were in town?"

"I like to hear Mel playing the drums. It makes this house sound alive."

"I'm going for a run."

| Sara's feet crunched through the leaves along the side of the road as she urged herself to keep going. She always found the first five minutes of a run difficult, and they were especially tough this morning. Her hips and knees were tight, her legs,

along with her heart, heavy and reluctant to pump. But Sara was good at pushing herself and persevered. Once at cruising pace, the heaviness dissipated and she felt lighter. She would run long to hang onto the lightness.

The path along the shore hadn't changed since the last time she'd been here, eight years ago, the morning after that final argument with her grandfather—two nights after Melanie left, one night after Abby's departure. He'd sat in his wingback chair behind his desk, a tumbler of Scotch in his hand.

"Both your sisters are gone, Sara. But they'll be back. You'll see."

He handed her a cheque for five thousand dollars.

"What's this for?"

"It's the same amount I gave the other two. See what you can do with it."

"No thanks. I'll find a job in the city."

"You've got a business degree. Create your own job. You're the smart one. The others are just like your mother. She got her hooks into Jake, trapped him into a loveless marriage. Don't mourn her, Sara. She was a conniving party girl, a harlot who ruined my son's life."

Sara's response was silence, except for the slammed door. She stayed up all night packing. In the morning, she went for her run, then loaded her brand-new Mustang and drove away, vowing never to return.

Now Sara reached the small bandstand at the centre of Lakefront Park, and she did a few laps of the park. She came to a stop when she looked up and, in the distance, saw the bluff where the Corvette had left the road. The concrete barrier the town built around the bluff's sharp curve after the accident was still there. Her other grandfather, Mayor Watson, harangued the town council for over a year, refusing to step down from office until the barrier was installed. A week after he resigned, he had a heart attack and the three sisters were dressed up for yet another funeral.

Sara turned away from the bluff and walked through the town, snaking up and down the tree-lined residential streets, past the hotel with the beer store still right beside it. Then came the hockey arena, and the Stay 'n Play arcade with the silver mechanical horse she'd ridden so often, pleading with her father for a quarter every time they walked by it. The horse was still there, looking like a museum piece now.

Just past the arcade, Sara came to the bank. She asked the teller if the bank manager was available. The teller led Sara into a small office, indicated that she should sit down, and then seated herself behind the desk. She smiled at Sara's unspoken question.

"Yes, I'm the manager, too. It's a small branch. We multitask here."

Sara fidgeted in her chair. "I'm not sure how to explain this, but I'm..."

"You don't have to explain. Earl told me to expect you, Sara. I have the signature cards right here."

The teller-manager watched as Sara signed. "Still the quiet type, I see. You don't remember me, do you?"

Sara studied the face. It was vaguely familiar. "Are you the kid that fell off the roof of our boathouse and broke her leg? Kelly?"

"Carrie. Yes, that was me. Mr. Smart banned me from the premises after that. How are Abby and Mel?"

"They seem fine. Abby has two sons. Mel has a bigger set of drums."

Carrie laughed. "Tell them I'm looking forward to seeing them both again." She stood up. "We're all done here. I'll see you out."

Sara walked to her parents' old house. Yet another FOR SALE sign graced the front yard, staked into the lawn. The house must have been bought and sold a few times over the years, because it looked as if opposing forces had tried to renovate it. A small addition painted forest-green was on one side. On the other, another addition was covered with faded cedar siding. Sara was surprised at how calm she felt. She'd expected to experience pangs of anguish when she saw their former home, but what she felt most right now was hunger, so she headed for home, breaking into a slow jog that picked up speed as she went.

| In the parlour, Andrew struggled as his mother tied an old pair of men's trousers around his waist with a piece of rope.

"This is a dumb costume. I want to be Spiderman."

"We don't have a Spiderman costume, so you get to be a tramp."

Standing next to his brother, Adam wore a similar pair of trousers, also fastened with rope. "Why do I have to be a tramp too? We can't be the same thing."

"Yes, you can. I found these two hats and some old suit jackets."

"It's a lame costume, Mom."

"Here's the best part. We can stuff these handkerchiefs with newspaper and tie them onto sticks that you can sling over your shoulders. Then, when I smudge dirt all over your faces, you'll be great little tramps."

Adam groaned. "Nobody goes out as tramps anymore, Mom. I want to be a hockey player."

"Unfortunately, there's no hockey equipment lying around this place, so that's out."

"Then I won't go."

"Fine. You stay here and hand out candy to all the other kids who come to the door."

"Okay, I'll be a tramp. But I won't be a happy one."

"That'll be perfect, because tramps aren't very happy."

Mel's voice came from the door. "I don't think we have tramps in the world anymore, Abby. We have homeless people."

Adam and Andrew wailed together: "I don't want to be a homeless person."

Abby shot Mel a dirty look, then turned back to her sons.

"Of course you don't want to be homeless. Nobody wants to be homeless. Tramps are different. They're from another time, when it was an adventure to roam from town to town, catching trains going anywhere in the middle of the night."

"That's right," Mel said. "Tramps were a bunch of rich guys out for a good time."

"Please, Mel. You're not helping."

Sara came in, breathless. She leaned against the parlour door and took a swig from her water bottle.

"Well?" said Abby, indicating the boys. "What do you think?"

"Seriously?" said Sara. "Homeless costumes for your kids?"

And the wailing began again.

| Abby didn't speak to either of her sisters for a full twenty-four hours. When Sara and Mel came into the kitchen seeking dinner the next night, Abby and the boys had already eaten.

"Get your own. I'm not your cook."

Once the boys had gone to bed, Sara and Mel tried again.

"We're sorry about the costume stuff. How long are you going to stay mad?"

"The deal was that you both have to be nice to my boys. That includes not undermining me as their mother."

Sara held up a bottle of wine. "We brought a peace offering."

Mel pulled another two bottles from behind her back. "Did you know this place has a wine cellar?"

"No. And we're probably not supposed to touch it," said Abby.

"Earl never said anything about a wine cellar," said Melanie. "And we're not going to touch the wine. We're going to drink it."

An hour later, the sisters had finished the first bottle. Mel opened the second.

"That looks familiar," said Sara. "And it's probably ancient. I think Dad used to like that wine."

"I envy you," said Abby to Sara as Mel poured another round.

"What the hell for?"

"Your memories of Mom and Dad. You can still see and hear them. Their voices are fading for me."

"I envy you both," said Mel. "Both their faces and voices have grown dim for me. Sometimes I feel like I never heard or saw them at all."

"Sometimes I feel like that too," said Sara. "But other times, it's as if they're right beside me. When I ran past the bandstand in town yesterday, I felt like Dad was just behind me, letting me win our fake race as usual."

They were on the third bottle of wine when they heard footsteps in the hall.

"Sorry to startle you, ladies. Random visit. I knocked, but apparently not loud enough. How are you managing?" Earl eyed the wine bottles on the table.

" We'd offer you a drink, but we're almost out," laughed Abby.

"Didn't I mention that the wine cellar is off-limits?"

"No, you didn't. And it wasn't locked," said Sara.

"I advise you to keep clear heads. Alcohol is not the best way to get through this experience."

"But it can help. I'm glad you dropped by," said Melanie. " You never told us what happened to Gramps. He was old, but not ancient. Why did he die?"

Earl shifted from one foot to the other. "My apologies. I should have mentioned that. We haven't received the official report yet, but the doctor suspects it was heart failure."

With that, he bowed to the sisters and left the room.

" Was it my imagination, or did Earl hesitate before answering that question?" asked Sara.

"I didn't notice anything," said Abby, draining her glass.

"Me neither," said Mel. "He seemed his usual smooth self to me." She slapped her forehead with her hand. "Crap. It's supposed to snow tomorrow. I should've asked about the snowmobile in the garage. Maybe I can catch him."

A minute later she was back, shaking her head. " That man disappears into thin air. Does anyone know where he lives?"

| Winter arrived two days after Halloween. Six inches of snow fell in two hours, burying pumpkins, bicycles, canoes, and gardens not yet readied for their seasonal hibernation. The

snow continued through November into December. The sisters spent most of their time shovelling the driveway.

Between blizzards, they made the rounds in town, looking for jobs. Their timing was bad. Jobs in a lakeside community are plentiful in summer, not in fall and winter. The only offer they had was a job-sharing position at The Perry Pond Café, owned and managed by Mrs. Cooper, whom they'd hardly seen since the day they arrived.

She eyed the three sisters standing at her café counter. "Okay, you're hired. Weekends only. One day each, Friday, Saturday, and Sunday. God knows, I don't want you all at the same time. Pick your own days. I don't care which one of you shows up. No free food."

Mel took the first shift. That night, she bounced through the kitchen door. "I think Mrs. Cooper and Earl are getting it on."

"Mel! Watch what you say around the boys."

"That's ridiculous," said Sara. "All that drumming is shaking your brains loose."

"Call me crazy, but he ate dinner at the café tonight. Mrs. Cooper served him herself. I saw them whispering to each other. And now there are footsteps in the snow up to the cabin. And a man's fedora on the bench by the door. That's why Earl appears and disappears so quickly. He doesn't trudge down the driveway. He dives into the gatekeeper's cabin for a hayroll."

"What's a hayroll, Mom?" asked Adam.

"Mel!" Abby scooted the boys from the kitchen and slammed the door behind her.

Sara rooted through the refrigerator. "Christ! Those damn kids ate all my yogurt."

| The next weekend, Abby rushed into the kitchen after her café shift. "Guess who sat down at the counter today?"

Mel and Sara couldn't be bothered to look up, much less guess.

"Robot-man! In jeans and a T-shirt, with no sunglasses. His eyes are blue. And he can smile. He's kind of cute. His name is Calvin. As in Klein. And guess what else?"

Still no guesses.

"You two are no fun. He calls Mrs. Cooper Mom!"

"How is that possible?" said Melanie. "We never saw him when we lived here."

"We were away at boarding school most of the time. And Mrs. Cooper was only the daytime housekeeper. She didn't live here. How were we supposed to know she had a kid?"

"You two are insane," said Sara. "Next you'll be trying to convince me that Robot-man calls Earl Dad."

Melanie and Abby stared at each other, their eyes widening. "Oh. My. God."

| The winter days were short and the evenings long. The evenings grew even longer when the sisters realized that they had depleted their wine supply.

"Why would a man with thirty million dollars have only thirty bottles in his wine cellar?" said Melanie.

"We'll have to do without from now on," said Abby. "The bank statement came today."

"I don't want to see it. I've grown allergic to bank statements," said Sara.

Drum sounds came from upstairs. Discordant, clashing, crashing drum sounds.

"Jesus, Abby," said Melanie. "How many times do I have to tell you? Keep those boys away from my drums."

Melanie ran upstairs. The sounds stopped. Minutes later, she was back, followed by two sullen boys.

"Why so mean, Mel?" said Abby. "Instead, maybe you could teach the boys how to play."

The boys brightened. Mel pursed her lips, thinking.

"Please don't. It's bad enough having you pounding those things every day. At least you're good," said Sara, muttering a curse under her breath that came out louder than she intended.

"Aunt Sara said the F word, Mom."

"Yeah, can we say the fuck word, too?"

Abby banished her older sister from the parlour. Sara wasn't ready for sleep, so she wandered down the hall to her grandfather's office. She plopped down into Jacob's big chair, swivelled a few times, and ran her hands over the leather writing surface. Then she reached down and pulled at a desk drawer. It was locked, as was the one on the other side. And the file drawers in his credenza. Earl knew her well.

The oiled ancestors watched from their portraits as Sara browsed through her grandfather's bookshelves. They were filled with classics, books with titles most people had heard of, but probably not many had read. *The Count of Monte Cristo*, *The Maltese Falcon*, *For Whom the Bell Tolls*, *The Grapes of Wrath*, *The Adventures of Huckleberry Finn*, *Robinson Crusoe*, *Treasure Island*, *The Red Badge of Courage*, *Lonesome Dove*, *A Farewell to Arms*, *The Great Gatsby*. Sara knew her grandfather would have read them all. She suppressed a laugh when she realized he didn't own one female-authored book.

"What the heck," Sara said aloud, as she pulled out *Moby-Dick*, blew the dust off, and settled back into Jacob's chair, with only one glance up at the walls. The ancestors could watch all they wanted. They didn't bother her. From that evening on, Jacob's office became her retreat.

| Winter finally ended. Six months had passed, the halfway point of their captivity. Carrie, the bank manager, had become a regular visitor, hanging out in the kitchen. One night, she advised the sisters that their original bank balance of one hundred thousand dollars was down to sixty thousand. She didn't have to remind them that their combined income per month was negligible. They needed a new plan. That night, they brainstormed at the dinner table.

"You could start a Spiderman camp," said Adam. "We could get all the kids in town here and teach them how to climb walls."

"Except we don't know how to climb walls, honey," said Abby.

"How about a drumming school! We'll get a hundred drum sets, put them in that old guesthouse, and Aunt Mel could teach everyone," said Andrew.

Sara groaned.

"Wait a sec. That's it!" said Abby. "The guesthouse. Spring is here. It'll be tourist season soon. There are five bedrooms in there. We'll open the guesthouse as a bed and breakfast."

Sara started to shake her head, but stopped. "Hmm. That's not a bad idea. Getting it ready will be a lot of work. The guest-house has been closed for years."

Melanie was eager. "We can do it. That's exactly what we need. Physical labour to shake off this winter malaise."

The clean-up wasn't easy. They had to kill spiders, set mouse traps, get rid of mould. To their surprise, they discovered they were a good working team. Melanie took the shutters down from the windows and painted them. Abby vacuumed all the mattresses, deodorized them with baking soda, and set them outside in the sun. She also prepared the bedding, planned a breakfast menu, and filled the freezer with home-baked muffins. Sara placed ads in the local paper and created a pamphlet she posted on bulletin boards in town. Carrie stopped by to offer moral support and help the sisters determine profitable room rates.

An umbrella of something resembling happiness settled over the group during the construction phase. The sisters recruited Calvin to put in new lighting, install new faucets in the bathrooms, repair the porch, and get the fireplace in the common room working. Calvin got the boys involved as helpers. They were uncharacteristically attentive when he taught them each how to use a hammer and enthralled when he built a bonfire to burn the construction debris. As the work progressed, Sara watched Abby, Melanie, and Carrie assist Calvin, tripping over themselves to be the first one to hand him a level or a wrench or the right nail.

"Isn't he wonderful?" said Abby on her way to fetch Calvin a coffee.

"Terrific," said Sara. "I feel another nephew coming on."

Sara wasn't surprised when Abby kept walking as if she hadn't heard. But she was surprised when Abby stopped and turned around.

"Here's a thought, sis," said Abby. "Why don't you give your uterus a workout? You might turn into a nicer person."

| They welcomed their first customers in the middle of June. A full house. The first day and night were a success. In the

morning, their guests raved about the fresh air and the breakfast. But the next day brought rain. A deluge. The roof leaked.
The sisters rushed to mop floors and place buckets under drips.
The rain stopped that afternoon, but the electricity went out
when several guests turned on hair dryers at the same time.
Abby and Melanie went to find Calvin. Sara found the electrical
box, flipped the breakers back on, and asked their guests to use
one small appliance at a time.

To compensate for these inconveniences, they provided a
complimentary cheese plate and brandy that night, serving
the treats beside a cozy fire in the common room. This was an
instant hit. Their guests emerged from their rooms and soon
many pairs of tired wet feet luxuriated in the new shag rug
in front of the fireplace. Sara, Abby, and Melanie reminded
everyone to ensure the fire was out before the last person
turned in for the night.

A few hours later, the smoke detectors went off. The fire
department arrived within minutes and extinguished the
blaze, while the sisters wrapped their guests in blankets from
the main house. Mrs. Cooper emerged from the cabin to
observe the commotion. "Smart sisters, my ass," she muttered.
Moments later, Earl appeared too, observed the scene, and
disappeared again.

The fire was out, but the guesthouse was uninhabitable. The
sisters called other hotels in the area to secure rooms for their
customers.

They'd now spent almost all their money and had nothing to
show for it.

| The blackened, smoky guesthouse permeated their moods for the rest of the summer. The sisters resumed their shifts at Mrs. Cooper's café, where Sara took pleasure in watching a courtship blossom between Calvin and Carrie. Abby and Melanie did not find this development as enjoyable.

June evenings at the mansion were light-filled and long. Melanie dragged her drums out to the dock and played "Wipeout" with the lake as audience. Abby puttered in the garden. Sara read more of her grandfather's books. As she did, her fingers toyed with the pulls on the desk's locked drawers. One night, she couldn't stand the restrictive feel of those locks any longer.

Breaking into the drawers was easy after a quick trip to the garage for a crowbar. The file drawers were empty. The desk's side drawers were also empty. But, in the slim centre drawer, Sara found a folder of newspaper clippings under a blank pad of paper. They were yellowed and brittle, like dried leaves that had been pressed in the pages of a heavy book. Sara handled them with care as she spread them out on the desktop. She read every word, memorizing the headlines: CAR MAGNATE'S WIFE DROWNS. MAYOR DENIES AFFAIR. FAMILY LAKE CURSE CONTINUES. BROKE & HEARTBROKEN MAYOR DROPS DEAD.

| With school out, Adam and Andrew spent their time between the beach and the town. Twice, they were banned from the arcade for stealing—the first time was for a week, but the second ban was for the whole summer. This stretched Abby's gentle nature to the limit. Furious, she prohibited the boys from leaving the yard, a punishment felt by as much by the sisters

as the boys. They soon tired of kicking a soccer ball around or throwing stones from the dock into the lake. Despite warnings from their mother and aunts, the boys repeatedly tried to climb the ladder up to the mansion's turret roof.

One hot July afternoon, Andrew slipped and fell as he made his way down the ladder. The only person who heard Andrew's cries was Earl, who emerged from the gatekeeper's cabin and rushed Andrew to the doctor's office in town, Adam trailing along.

Abby came home from her shift at the café to find Sara and Melanie pacing the veranda. " What's wrong?"

"Don't panic, Abby, but we're not sure where the boys are," said Sara.

Before Abby could react, Earl returned, the boys in tow. Andrew's arm was in a sling.

"I called from the clinic, but no one answered. It's a broken collarbone, I'm afraid," said Earl, looking at Abby. " The boys shouldn't be on the turret roof. And their mother should be watching them."

Abby's face turned red. "I was at work, Earl. You know, the job where I make in an hour what you make in a nanosecond."

She whirled around to Sara. " Where were you? I asked you to watch them."

"I did, but not every minute. They were kicking a soccer ball in the yard, so I went into Grandfather's office to read. It's cooler in there. Why don't you yell at Mel? She was on the veranda when I left. And probably encouraged them to climb up there in the first place."

"Piss off, Sara. The boys seemed happy playing ball, so I went upstairs to drum and fell asleep instead. I'm sorry."

Melanie turned on Earl. "Why didn't you try calling again? We've spent the last three hours scouring every inch of this place. You scared the crap out of us."

| And so it went for the rest of the summer. Until one sultry August evening, when the sisters met in the kitchen after the boys had gone to bed. Sara pulled out the latest bank statement. "We're down to our last thousand dollars. Any ideas?"

"I'm too hot to think," said Abby.

"I hate to say this, but we're now the defeated dumb sisters," said Melanie. "We're finished. Done like dinner."

"What's that smell?" said Sara.

Melanie would remember that the explosion came before the flames. Abby would remember the flames first, then the explosion. Sara would claim that the explosion and the flames happened simultaneously. But they would all agree that when they raced outside, the back of the gatekeeper's cabin was on fire, with smoke pouring out its cracked windows. Adam and Andrew darted from the darkness and flung their arms around Abby's waist. "We're sorry! It was an accident!"

Melanie and Sara pounded on the cabin's front door. Within seconds, Mrs. Cooper emerged, followed by two men: Earl Stanfield and Jacob Smart.

As if under a spell, the sisters stood transfixed at the sight of their dead grandfather, until Sara strode over and punched the old man in the gut.

| For the second time that summer, firefighters had doused a blaze at the Smart property. After it was under control, the fire chief explained that the boys had been playing with matches

behind the cabin, near a pile of dried grass and a can of gasoline for the lawn mower. He was stern in his reprimand. "You're lucky no one was killed."

An hour later, Jacob sat at one end of his kitchen table. Andrew and Adam sat at the other, eyes wide as they studied the grey-haired man in front of them. Sara, Abby, and Melanie stood near the door, their arms folded across their chests. Behind Jacob stood Mrs. Cooper and Earl, who attempted an explanation.

"We apologize for the ruse. It seemed the only way to bring you all together again. We didn't think you would last this long."

"I can't believe you did this to us," said Abby. "Dangled the thirty million like bait, like we're. . .mindless pets."

"The thirty million is an inflated figure," said Earl. "We exaggerated the amount as incentive for you to stay."

"So there is no money?" said Melanie.

"The estate's value has been compromised over the last few years, but it's not all gone."

Sara glowered at Earl as she pointed to her grandfather. "Why are you doing the talking? Is he so old and feeble that he can't speak for himself?"

"There's no need to be rude, Sara," said Jacob. "I'm neither feeble nor old. I'm only seventy-six. But I've come to realize that I've made some mistakes. This. . .situation is one of them. You're right. It should be me apologizing for the hoax. And I do. I take full responsibility. My intentions were good. I wanted my family back."

"First you're dead, then you're alive, and now you want your family back?" said Melanie. "I'm out of here."

"Me too," said Abby. "Come on, boys. Let's pack."

Sara held her hand up. " Wait. We should stay. At least for a while. We need some answers."

" To what?" said Abby.

"Nobody move. I'll be right back," said Sara, leaving the room.

A minute later, she returned, the yellowed newspaper clippings she'd found in Jacob's desk in her hand.

"I broke into Grandfather's desk one night." Sara stifled Earl's protest with a flash of her eyes. " This is what I found." She read out the headlines, finishing with FAMILY LAKE CURSE CONTINUES, then held it up so everyone in the room could see the picture of their parents, Jake and Janet, smiling on their wedding day.

" You want peace, Grandfather? You want your family back?" said Sara, sliding the clippings across the table to Jacob. " You can start by talking to us about these."

Limbo

I'D BE THIRTY-EIGHT YEARS OLD NOW. I'd have a wife and a couple of kids. And a dog. A huge panting dog that came when I called him. By this time, my dad might have opened his ears enough to hear what I say to him. My mom would still tell me to put a sweater on. My sister Charlotte would still kick my ass at Trivial Pursuit. I sucked at that game, especially in the Sports and Leisure category. "Wrong again, Rog. Are you sure you're a football player?"

She never called me Roger. Always Rog. Always with a laugh. Char's laugh was big, even when we were kids. Throaty. Lusty. Its sound was home to me.

On that last day, I was in a hole—a dark clammy tight hole. The ache in my brain throbbed all the way down to my toes. My chest and ribs were so tight that by the end of the night, I couldn't breathe. I didn't plan it. The idea started as a pesky germ that grew into a way out. A roll of duct tape appeared in my hands. I wound it around the tail of the exhaust pipe, sealed the windows, and crawled into the back of the Econoline. I didn't think about my family or my friends. I didn't think about anything. Too bad clarity comes only in retrospect. Back then, all I saw was blackness. The germ beckoned me, disguised as relief. The welcome end.

I didn't know it wouldn't be the end. I didn't know that I'd float in ether, witnessing the aftermath of me, that I'd be locked in limbo for the next twenty years.

I am a reluctant haunter. I don't want to haunt them, don't want them to think about me at all. I want to be fully erased. Like I never existed.

Jean's Slice

The day after his seventieth birthday, Stan Andrews told Jean to get the house they'd lived in for forty-five years ready to sell. He'd bought a cottage in a small lakeside town, and they were moving. Jean pulled her hands from the sink and wiped them on a tea towel as she turned to where her husband sat, still in his place at their kitchen table. She had much to say, but chose a silent eyebrow message instead.

"Don't look at me like that, Jeanie. The new place is a five-minute walk from the water. Trust me. You'll like it."

When Stan and Jean left their home for the last time, they followed the moving van up the street. Jean asked Stan to drive slowly because the packed boxes of good china were in the back seat of the sedan. One neighbour waved from her front lawn. Jean raised her hand in a farewell salute.

To her surprise, Jean discovered that she enjoyed living in Peregrine Lake. After only a few days, she was calling it Perry Pond like everyone else. Back in the city, she'd moved through her daily routine without thinking, sometimes momentarily surprised to find herself standing in the grocery store or at the pharmacy counter. She lost track of entire days.

Here in Perry Pond, Jean's days felt fresh, even though the town wasn't. Everything and everyone in it was mature, perpetually ripe, on the edge of decay; not yet deteriorating, merely preserved. Perhaps that's what Jean relished the most: the feeling that she'd stepped back twenty or thirty years, to a simpler time.

She and Stan spent most afternoons wandering along Main Street. People stopped to say hello and chat. And Stan responded to them. Jean had never seen Stan engage in small talk before.

It happened six months later, in the hardware store, in the absence of a heartbeat. Jean was standing beside Stan in the power tool aisle, listening to her husband and the store manager discuss the benefits of one drill brand over another.

"The only thing that matters is power," said Stan.

With that, he crumpled to the floor. The manager shouted for the cashier to call an ambulance, and ran to the pharmacy next door. The pharmacist tried to revive Stan for forty-five minutes.

Many hours later, Jean sat in her kitchen, two sealed brown envelopes on the table in front of her. Right after their move, at her insistence, she and Stan had faced each other across their dining-room table, pens in hand, sheets of paper waiting for words, him glowering at her.

"Why are we doing this?"

"Because I want to."

"I don't see the point. We already have wills."

"This is for anything else you want me to know."

They wrote in silence. In her letter to him, Jean wrote that she was grateful for his constant support. She said she didn't want any flowers at her funeral, that perhaps he could donate money to the Youth Emergency Shelter on her behalf instead, that Charlotte should have her wedding ring and the gold watch he'd given her for her sixtieth birthday. In closing, she thanked him for their life together and signed it "all my love, Jean." When she finished writing, she looked up. Stan was already sealing his envelope.

Now Jean opened it and pulled out Stan's letter. His erratic slanted scrawl, almost illegible because he'd been a natural lefty forced to use his right hand, filled only half the page. His words were a list of instructions: how to start the lawn mower, that she should have the oil in the car changed twice a year, and where she'd find the key to their safety deposit box (in the shed, under the workbench). His last sentence was a reminder to return the safety deposit box key, or the bank would charge her for it. The page was unsigned.

| The morning of Stan's funeral, the church ladies appeared on her doorstep right after nine. They took over the main floor of her house, refusing Jean's help, leaving her nothing to do but wait upstairs. She sat on the edge of her bed, listening to noises rise from the kitchen as the ladies prepared sandwiches and fruit trays and dessert plates.

In the five days since Stan's death, a calmness had come over Jean. The feeling confused her. Each day, a different cluster of new neighbours stopped by to pay their respects.

"We're so sorry for your loss."

"Is there anything you need? Anything at all?"

"You're handling this situation very well, Jean. So calm at such a difficult time."

" Thank you. I've never been the hysterical type." Jean laughed when she said that. She meant it as a joke to lighten the moment. What she didn't say was that she knew what hysteria felt like, and this wasn't it.

But it wasn't grief either, and that's what made her uncomfortable. She should be shattered, lost, incomplete, as if part of herself had been rudely amputated—but she wasn't. For four and a half decades, she'd been Stan's wife. She had to feel *something*. Yet, here she was, sitting on the edge of their bed, with what remained of her life looming ahead like an unanswered question, feeling nothing.

When she walked into the church that afternoon, Jean saw her Perry Pond neighbours filling every pew. The funeral service was dignified and mercifully short, but the reception afterwards seemed endless. For several hours, Jean's small living room was crowded with mourners, many of whom she'd met only a few times, some whose names she couldn't remember. Circulating through this friendly flock of people, she felt their gentle touches on her arm, saw their sad lingering gazes, and accepted their well-intended comments.

"Didn't know him long, but felt like I knew him well," said one man. Jean recognized him from the bank on Main Street.

"Nice man, your husband. Quiet, but nice," said the lady from the post office.

"I'm so sorry. You must be devastated," said a woman wearing a blue hat adorned with a peacock feather in its brim. Jean had no idea who she was, and moved on quickly.

Eventually, the mass of humanity in her living room dwindled. Before they left, the church ladies washed all the cups, wiped up the crumbs from the tables and made Jean a pot of tea. Moira Black, the local coffee maven, was the last to leave.

Jean liked Moira, admired her wild mane of dyed red hair and endless wardrobe of flowing rainbow-coloured caftans. Well into her seventies, Moira still went to work every day at Bean There Done That, a comfy café in the centre of town, where townsfolk gathered to eat homemade soup and linger over pungent fair-trade coffee from Sumatra.

"You sure you'll be all right tonight, Jeanie? I can stay."

"I'll be fine. Thanks for everything, Moira. I'll drop by the café soon."

Jean waved Moira off. Finally alone, she slumped against the door and looked at the flower arrangements crowding her living room. Vases of all sizes filled every tabletop, each blossom radiating vibrant good health. Jean had never told anyone, not even her family, how much she disliked cut flowers. They would be lovely for a few days, maybe more, but decay was inevitable. Sometimes she was tempted to throw them out right away, but she never did. Instead, she resigned herself to days of watching them fade, wither, and droop. She was relieved when they died, so she could wrap their decomposing corpses in newspaper and bury them in the garbage can.

The guest book from the church and the basket of condolence cards sat on the coffee table. Several white rose petals had fallen on the guest book from a nearby vase. Jean picked up an unopened card, but set it back down again. Over on the side table, the message light on her phone flashed. Probably another call from Brisbane, another apologetic long-distance call during which Charlotte would berate herself for not being with her mother during this terrible time, and Jean would attempt to soothe her daughter's guilt. But Jean had no more soothing left in her tonight, so this message would have to wait until tomorrow. She kicked off her black pumps, sank down onto the sofa, and pulled a blanket up over her legs.

| She was still on the sofa the next morning when the first gusts of a storm began soon after dawn. The wind grew steadily over the next few hours. By noon, the branches on the pine and oak trees surrounding her house were swaying, brushing against the roof and walls. Jean didn't move. She felt more immobilized than tired, her entire body held still by inertia. Except her brain, which wouldn't stop swirling a sea of thoughts, all with a common theme: *Why don't I feel anything?*

By late afternoon, the wind had intensified and the rain started. Jean heard the shutters she'd helped Stan paint last month rattle against the siding. The room grew dark. She stretched up to turn on the table lamp and dropped back down onto the sofa. Her head throbbed. An ache at her left temple drummed in time with her heartbeat. Raindrops splashed against the window, blurring her view of the front garden.

Soon the rain turned to hail, and wind howled all around the house. Jean pulled the blanket up to her chin and looked at the ceiling, waiting to hear shingles fly off the roof. A series of lightning flashes filled the room, like disco strobes, the ones from that John Travolta movie she and Stan had watched more than once.

Then came sounds of wood splintering. A lightning strike? She sniffed the air for any hint of smoke. Seconds later, a ferocious clap of thunder shook the house. This time, Jean pulled the blanket over her head. The light flickered out and the room went dark. Jean fell asleep again.

An insistent tapping woke her. At first she thought it was one of those loose boards on the porch, the ones Stan said he would fix next week, but the tapping turned into rapping, growing louder until Jean realized it was coming from the front door. She dragged herself off the sofa, lurching on her first steps as if drunk or Frankenstein or both. The rapping came again. *Who could it be? Stan? One of the kids? Did they forget their keys again?*

Jean opened the door. A gale of wind roared through, whipping the handle out of her hand, and blowing a drenched visitor into her house. She staggered backward. The soggy figure fell to the floor. Jean used her full body weight to close the door against the wind. Her visitor struggled to his feet. In the dark, Jean couldn't see which of her neighbours this person was.

"Good grief! Are you okay?"

The dark shape shook itself and wet drops splattered onto Jean.

"Good evening, ma'am. I'm sorry to bother you on a night like this."

She didn't know this voice, had never heard it before. The darkness that surrounded them deepened. Jean's hands grew clammy, as she tried to visualize a potential weapon within close range—a broom, a walking stick, anything pointy. The umbrella stand was nearby, but he stood between it and Jean.

"What do you want?" she asked.

"Do you need your knives sharpened?"

After a moment of stunned silence, Jean burst out laughing. The long hours of stillness melted away, and her body doubled over as she gave in to deep guffaws, during which the shadowy figure didn't move. When Jean's fit of laughter subsided, she opened the hall closet, pulled the flashlight down from the shelf, and shone it on her visitor.

He was somewhere between thirty and forty years old, with pale skin, ocean-blue eyes, and a shaggy but sparse goatee that didn't quite cover his chin. His tattered rain jacket and shabby running shoes were soaking wet. His face was impassive, his lips blue, and his body trembling. Jean wasn't sure what to do, but she couldn't send him away in this condition.

"Well, why not? What else can we do with this night? I'm sure I have some dull knives here somewhere. But let's get you warmed up first."

He shook off his pack and removed his wet coat and shoes.

Jean turned, pointing her beam of light toward the kitchen. "Follow me."

As she passed the sofa, Jean picked up the blanket and passed it to her shivering guest. At the kitchen door, she lit the table with the flashlight beam, and, with the blanket wrapped around his shoulders, her visitor sat down in Stan's usual chair.

Jean rested the flashlight on the counter. "The power could be off for a while, so I'd better conserve that battery," she said, lighting the emergency candles stored on her cookbook shelf. Silently thanking Stan for insisting they install a wood stove, she then started the process of lighting it.

"Nice stove you got there." The stranger's voice was low and hoarse.

"Thanks. It's new. I'm not used to it yet."

Jean had never done this by herself before, but she'd watched Stan do it every day since they got it. She placed two logs on a pile of kindling and crumpled newspaper, then struck a wooden match along the side of its box. The flame flared up immediately.

"Good work," he said. "Seems like you know what you're doing."

Soon the room felt warmer and Jean felt her muscles relax somewhat. Her visitor was still shivering, so Jean made hot chocolate on the stovetop and poured two cups.

"I hope you're feeling warmer."

"Getting there." Still, his hands shook as they circled the mug Jean handed him.

"Do you have a name?"

"Slice."

"Slice?"

"Yeah. Everyone calls me Slice."

"Why?"

"Because after I've sharpened a knife, it'll slice through anything...like a noontime sunbeam through cold butter."

Jean studied his face, but it was expressionless.

"Is your family from around here?" she asked, hoping he was the banker's second cousin, or maybe the mayor's sister's son.

"I have no family."

"No one?"

He shook his head. "Never had a father. My mom drowned herself when I was ten. Paddled into the middle of the lake, tied sandbags to her ankles, and rolled out of the canoe."

Jean heated up some chicken noodle soup, toasted two big dinner rolls, and unwrapped the desserts left over from the funeral reception. Her guest consumed everything she put in front of him. Jean felt quite pleased with herself for handling this process without electricity, and thought how her efficiency would have surprised Stan. He never let Jean do anything he deemed too difficult for her.

"Where did you grow up, Slice?"

"About twenty miles from here. After my mom died, my uncle took me in. As soon as I turned eighteen, he kicked me out."

"That wasn't very nice of him."

"I probably wasn't the world's best nephew."

"Where do you live now?"

"In the cheapest motel I can find. I like to get up and go."

"Do you get lonely?"

"Nope," he said. "Do you?"

Outside, the wind bellowed and the shutters rattled against the house. Reflected in the window, Jean saw Slice studying her in return. Her breath caught in her throat.

I have a complete stranger sitting at my table. He could be anybody. A criminal. Or a pervert, as Stan would say.

She heard her husband's voice inside her head, heard the exact words he would use right now: "What in tarnation do you think you're doing?"

Maybe this is what my life is going to be like from now on. I'll do irrational things, and people will shake their heads and say what a sensible person Jean used to be before Stan passed on.

Jean swiped a dishcloth across the counter. A lightning bolt flashed, and the simultaneous thunderclap made her jump. Seconds later, a splintering crash echoed through the house. From the window, she saw a thick branch from their willow tree lying on the driveway. The chaos outside matched the chaos she felt inside herself, and Jean could only deal with chaos when she was alone. She needed her visitor to leave.

"Maybe this isn't a good time to have my knives sharpened."

Another thudding crash came from the front yard. Jean ran into the living room. Out the window, she saw a spruce tree lying across the porch steps.

"That was my favourite tree," she said. How strange it looked lying on the ground, felled by a surprising force from the very sky it had reached for each day of its life.

Slice emerged from the kitchen, still swallowing a piece of cake, and started putting on his still-wet shoes and jacket. Lightning flashed, with thunder right on top of it. Almost immediately, another bolt and clap exploded right above them, followed by a series of thuds as more branches hit the ground. Jean cringed and peered at the ceiling again. Surely the next tree to fall would hit the house.

Slice shrugged into his pack and Jean opened the door to let him out. Wind and rain pelted into the room. Jean closed the door again. Her mind urged her not to say the words even as they came out of her mouth. "I suppose you could rest on the sofa until the storm passes."

He smiled at her. His front teeth were crooked, as if he should have had braces when he was a child. He slid his pack off again, hung up his jacket, and shoved his shoes under the hall bench beside an old pair of Stan's work boots.

"Nice boots. They look sturdy."

A montage of family photos hung on the wall above the bench.

"Expecting him home soon?" he asked, pointing to Stan.

Jean looked at the flower arrangements scattered around the room, at the pile of condolence cards sitting on the console table, and down at her good black suit, now rumpled from being on her body for two straight days. "Yes, any time now."

"Is this your daughter?"

Jean glanced at Charlotte, captured standing between her parents in a snapshot taken at the airport before she left after her last visit. *Could it be four years ago already?*

"Yes."

"Where is she?"

"On her way here."

Slice turned to the last picture, a high-school photo of a young man wearing a football jersey. This was a new addition to the montage. Less than a week after their son's death twenty years ago, Stan had removed all their pictures of Roger and thrown them in the garbage. The day before yesterday, Jean had retrieved this one from its hiding spot at the bottom of her sweater drawer and hung it on the wall.

"Who's this?"

"My son."

"Where is he?"

"He died."

"How?"

"Carbon monoxide poisoning."

"I tried that once. Someone saved me."

Jean eyed his dirty clothes. "I'll get you something to sleep in."

Using a flashlight to make her way upstairs and back, Jean returned with Stan's blue flannel robe, a T-shirt, and an old pair of sweat pants. She handed them to Slice. "I hope you'll find the sofa comfortable. I've slept on it myself a few times." She gestured toward the kitchen. "The bathroom is in the back. The toilet flusher is a little testy. Tends to stick."

Upstairs, Jean checked the bedroom window. The wind was louder up here. She closed the curtains to muffle the sounds of cracking branches. Only then did she shed her funeral wear. A pair of pajamas and a nightgown hung on the back of the closet door. Since Stan died, she'd worn the pajamas every night, wrapping herself in the Old Spice smell of her husband as she crawled into their bed. But sleep had been restless, elusive. As soon as she drifted off, her eyes would fly open. Then she'd doze off again only to wake up a short while later, the heavy cotton fabric of Stan's pajama bottoms tangled around her legs, her hands lost in the length of his arms.

Tonight, Jean left Stan's pajamas hanging on the back of the door and put on her nightgown. But her eyes refused to close. She considered reading, but didn't want to fall asleep with a candle burning or wear out the batteries in her flashlight, so she lay on her back, listening to the thunder and the wind and the questions in her head: *What will I do if he comes upstairs? What will I do tomorrow?* She took deep breaths, one after another after another. In and out. Out and in. *What will I do next week, next month, next year?*

Eventually her muscles gave in to stillness. The inertia returned, again immobilizing everything but her brain, which was all motion, flitting from last week to forty-five years ago, a slideshow playing in her head.

Jean wearing a cream-coloured suit and a pillbox hat as she and Stan stood in front of a solemn minister in an almost-empty chapel on the day they got married.

Jean wearing a sky-blue dress, holding an infant bundled in a blue blanket. Beside her, five-year-old Charlotte, dressed all in pink. Stan tall behind them, a football tucked under his arm.

Jean wearing a green and gold muffler around her neck as she and Charlotte sat in the grandstands at Roger's last football game. Stan had been pacing behind the team bench, calling out strategy to the coach: "Let him go long! You know he can throw that thing!"

Jean wearing a navy-blue sundress the day they scattered Roger's ashes beside the river. Her dress was blue because she didn't own anything black, and what did it matter anyway? Her beautiful towheaded boy was dead.

Jean woke with a start and listened. Between the storm's flashes and cracks came odd scraping sounds, rising from below, like metal on metal, or two stones rubbing together.

Slice. What was he doing?

Jean threw a robe over her nightgown, ventured to the top of the stairs, and peered over the railing. The sofa was empty. Flickering yellow light came from the kitchen, drawing her to it.

Candles glowed on the counter. Slice's pack lay open on the floor. On the table, all her knives were lined up according to length. He stood beside the table, bending over a large, grey sharpening stone, working on Stan's new meat cleaver, the one he'd bought the day before he died—the last purchase he ever made.

The candle-glow made the scene look like an old master's oil painting. She thought of a Rembrandt, all gold and yellow at the centre, flickering into shadows and darkness around the edges. Slice's shining face mesmerized Jean.

Then reality smashed the artistry. A strange man was in her kitchen in the middle of the night with an arsenal of weapons at his immediate disposal. He looked up.

"Got any more knives? Scissors, maybe?"

"No. You found them all."

Slice held up the meat cleaver. The blade gleamed as he raised it into the air. He ran his finger along the edge.

"Nice instrument you got here."

"It's brand new. Should have been sharp enough already."

" They're never sharp enough."

" There's cold butter in the refrigerator if you want to test the blades. At least I hope it's still cold with the power off this long. Good night again."

Back upstairs, Jean lay listening to the storm. Its thunder was softer now as it began to lose strength. How many more storms would she live through in her life? How many more strangers would put her in surprising situations? What would she do with the years she had left, years with no husband to tend to, no adult children living nearby, no grandchildren to babysit? She'd never expected to turn into a seventy-five-year-old woman with no family to look after. The thought that she might be alone one day had occurred to her over the years—after all, women do tend to outlive men—but that day was always far in the future.

| This time, the quiet woke her up. She opened the curtains. The sun was already high in the sky. Their normally pristine back-yard looked like the aftermath of a hurricane. And maybe that's what it was. Jean had never been in a hurricane, so she couldn't be sure, but she knew a mess when she saw one. Deck chairs she didn't recognize lay on their sides. The back porch planter sprawled broken on the ground. Downed branches, unrecognizable debris, and three unfamiliar canoes littered the lawn. Jean dressed and went downstairs.

The blanket was on the sofa, neatly folded on top of the pillow she'd provided her guest.

"Slice?"

His name sounded odd hanging in the lightness of the morning air.

Silence. Stan's robe and sweatpants hung by the front door, but his boots were no longer under the bench.

"Slice? Are you here?"

More silence. Outside, the spruce that had fallen across her front porch and the big branch behind Stan's car were gone. Piled beside the shed was a new stack of chopped wood. Next to the pile was Stan's axe, its blade gleaming in the sunlight.

Jean fiddled with the flower arrangements in her living room, plucking out a few blossoms already showing signs of deterioration. The phone rang. Jean rearranged two white lilies as she listened to her daughter's voice.

"I'm fine, Charlotte. Stop apologizing."

She straightened the photos on the wall.

"Yes, I was tired after the funeral. And we've had a bit of a storm, but today is a blue-sky day."

She touched Roger's face, brushed her hand across the lock of hair falling across his forehead.

"I really am just fine, dear. I'd rather you came out next spring, when you can spend some time here."

A neat row of knives lay on the kitchen table. Without that lineup of shiny blades and the stack of wood outside, Jean might have convinced herself that she'd dreamed her strange visitor. *He could have at least said goodbye.*

The note was on the table, nestled between the napkin holder and the sugar bowl, its message printed in large child-like letters.

"Sorry about your husband. The boots were my size. Thanks."

Jean's stomach growled. It was the first time she'd felt hungry since Stan's death. She decided to make herself an omelet and fetched an onion from the pantry. The pungent vegetable succumbed easily to the sharp knife, an instrument now infused with a renewed energy. Effortlessly, she sliced a pepper and glided through a tomato. Rather than grating the cheddar cheese, she slivered small chunks of it with a paring knife. As the omelet sizzled on the stove, Jean discovered that she was humming. She couldn't remember the last time she had hummed.

She set the table for one and turned on the small television in the corner, switching channels until she found a news program.

"Worst storm to hit the region in forty-five years..."

"Power has been restored to most of the lake area..."

A news anchor with shiny hair and a friendly voice continued to describe the storm's havoc as Jean ate, savouring each bite, until the news report switched to a breaking bulletin.

"Area police are searching for this man as a person of interest in a series of robberies. He's a Caucasian male with blue eyes. He carries a large pack..."

Slice stared out at Jean from his mug shot. She choked on her mouthful of egg and fell into a coughing fit. Then she hurried to the closet where she kept her purse. Her wallet was still inside, cash and credit card undisturbed. The image of Slice's face burnished gold in the candlelight filled her mind's eye, dissolving only when the phone rang.

"Jeanie! Wasn't that something! You okay?" Moira's sentences always sounded like they were punctuated with exclamation or question marks.

"Yes. Fine."

"Did you hear about that criminal on the loose? Have you seen anyone lurking around?"

"No, no one."

"Well, keep your eyes open and your door locked! I must run! A big tree fell right through the front window of the café!"

As Jean washed and dried her knives, she held each one up to the light and ran her finger along the flat edge of the cool metal blade. When she was done, she fetched her work gloves and headed outside to the mess in her backyard. She had to find the owners of those canoes.

Dad always called it assessment time. "Ah. Spring," he'd say, inhaling deep, exhaling with a blow. "Time to shake off the winter mould."

First we'd go on our annual fishing trip. I'd spend two days in the boat listening to Dad relive every play from his football days. Then it was time to sweat.

"Get working on those football muscles, boy. It's all in the conditioning. And there's no time like the present. Jump-start everyone else."

I knew the speech by heart and didn't object. It was easier to let him have his way. We'd work on my throwing arm. I'd toss the ball and he'd hurl it back. No matter how far the ball went, it was never long enough for him. Dad had a way of getting my running legs in shape, too. If I didn't toss the ball as far as he thought I could, I'd have to do ten laps around the field. Sometimes I threw it short on purpose. Running was a nice break. Sometimes, Char would run with me.

When I was little, maybe about four, I went into Char's room and drew on her walls with felt-tipped pens. Boy, was she mad. Started to ream me out. Mom stopped her. Said Char had a responsibility as a big sister. Instead of getting mad, Mom said, she should teach me. The next day, Mom went to the store and bought some paint. Char and I spent the afternoon repainting her bedroom walls. Never thought I'd say this, but I miss hanging out with my sister.

As Dad would say, Char is a "good egg." And I left her in a mess.

I did think about her once that night. Char was so cool and capable, I knew she would handle things after I was gone, that she'd look after Mom. Damn selfish thinking by the idiotic ass I was. Am. Will always be. An idiotic ass frozen at the height of his idiocy.

Orphan Sister

Charlotte told her mother not to pick her up at the airport.

"Don't drive all that way just to get me. I'll catch a bus to Peregrine Lake."

"Nonsense. I'd have to wait two hours longer to see you. I'll be there when you arrive."

After they reached cruising altitude, Charlotte reclined her seat, one notch back from the uncomfortable upright position. She wriggled her butt to settle in. The hop from Brisbane to Sydney had been uneventful, the takeoff from Sydney Airport smooth in clear morning skies. From her window at thirty-nine thousand feet, the Pacific Ocean looked like atmosphere. Her eyes searched for the horizon, but she couldn't pinpoint the exact spot where water became air.

As usual when she was sitting motionless while moving, whether it was in a car or a train or an airplane, Roger entered her thoughts. Today, his image flickered across the clouds, his long limbs sprawled on her bedroom floor, him looking up at the ceiling, hands behind his head, listening to the music that blared from her portable stereo. Her favourite song back then was Alannah Myles's "Black Velvet." Whenever the song ended, she replayed it.

"Again?" he said. "You're killing my ears. How about some Doobie Brothers?"

"What for? They're loud and old. You're too young to be stuck in the past."

Both dateless that Saturday night, they went to a movie, *The Silence of the Lambs*. At the worst parts, Charlotte buried her face in Roger's sleeve. She didn't sleep for the next three nights.

Their mother couldn't understand why Roger started calling his sister Clarice. "Come into my cage, Clarice. Come share some beans with me, Clarice." A few short months later, her brother was dead.

Long before her father's death last summer, Charlotte had felt like an orphan. She knew the sensation was ridiculous, perhaps even irrational. Losing her only sibling did not make her an orphan. Yet when she imagined what a real orphan might feel like, it was her: unmoored, teetering, struggling to find her balance on shifting ground. She worked hard to shed that feeling. On long walks, she'd thrust her arms out sideways, as if shaking off dead skin. It never worked. This was her reality. Charlotte felt orphaned by her brother's death and would prob- ably always be pissed off at him for abandoning her.

She looked at her watch. They'd been flying for forty- five minutes. Fifteen and half hours more to Vancouver, and another three-hour flight after that. She tried reading, but couldn't concentrate. She tried watching a movie, but the choices were an asinine romantic comedy or science fiction. She tried sleeping. Not a chance. That left her with nothing to do but think about the next month. She pulled out her notebook and wrote a list of conversation starters, things she could talk to her mother about. The list was short. *Was her favourite singer still Dean Martin? What had happened on* Coronation Street *in the last two decades? Was she lonely?*

Charlotte looked over what she'd written and crossed the last question off the list. Of course her mother was lonely. How could she not be? She rephrased it. *How are you managing all by yourself?* She tried to picture how her mother would look now. After a year of widowhood, she was probably pale, reclusive, reluctant to leave her house—the same as she'd been twenty years ago. Charlotte steeled herself for a long month of cajoling. She was determined to nudge Jean out of her comfort zone. Perhaps convince her to volunteer at the church, or join a bird-watching group.

Standing near the luggage carousel, Charlotte stood on her tiptoes scanning the crowd for her mother's face, for the neatly trimmed salt-and-pepper hair, for the grey raincoat she'd been wearing the last time. A blur burst through the crowd and engulfed her in a breath-defying bear hug. Her mother's voice laughed in her ear, but when Charlotte pulled back, she hardly recognized the woman holding onto her.

Jean's face was tanned, her eyes bright and clear. The pepper had disappeared from her hair, the salt having completely taken over. Instead of the controlled bob style Jean usually wore, this woman's shiny silver hair was loose and tousled, falling freely. She had a yellow and orange scarf wrapped around her neck, and green plumage dangled from her ears.

"Mom, you look so different. Are you wearing feather earrings?"

Jean took the handle of Charlotte's wheeled luggage with one hand, and her daughter's arm with the other. Outside, Charlotte was astonished when they stopped in front of a small red vehicle that looked far too much like a sports car. It couldn't be an actual sports car. Her mother would never drive one of those.

Jean gave her daughter an impish grin. "I bought myself a little treat."

During the two-hour drive, Charlotte hardly had to say a word. Jean chatted easily as she maneouvred her car through traffic and out onto the open road, then commented on the

farms, fields, and towns they passed. Charlotte didn't know
what surprised her more, the cheeriness of her mother's banter
or the casual confidence of her driving. The mother Charlotte
remembered preferred the passenger seat. She studied Jean's
profile. Her mother looked younger now than she had five years
ago. At one point during the drive, Charlotte heard humming.
She couldn't ever remember Jean humming. This daughter had
no idea what to say to the person who used to be her mother.

| Charlotte soon discovered that Jean's life as a widow wasn't
quiet or lonely. Her mother was busy, so busy that Charlotte
spent most mornings waiting for Jean to come home from a
volunteer shift at the library or a meeting with the town council
about the noise by-law.

In the afternoons, mother and daughter wandered along the
town's main street, Charlotte trailing after Jean, smiling politely
every time her mother stopped to introduce her to someone
new. They usually stopped at the Bean There Done That Café to
visit with the owner, Moira Black, Jean's new best friend. Moira
was a broad-shouldered busty woman, with dyed crimson hair
and a loud voice.

The first time they met, Moira looked at Charlotte up, down,
and sideways. "You're taller than I expected, more robust. Are
you sure you're Jean's daughter?"

Charlotte sputtered for an answer.

Moira let out a hearty laugh. "Just kidding, honey," she said,
with a pulled boxer's punch to Charlotte's shoulder. "You look
exactly like your mom. I'd have known you anywhere."

Charlotte wasn't sure she liked the easy intimacy of her
mother's friendship with Moira until the day she came downstairs
to find the two women doing yoga headstands against the

dining-room wall. In her entire life, Charlotte had never seen her mother do any kind of exercise other than walking.

"Wow," said Charlotte. "Look at you, Mom."

"You should try it yourself," said Jean, coming down from the wall. "It's so refreshing."

Moira righted herself, too. "You've got to loosen up those hips, girlfriend," she said, reaching over to move Charlotte's hips from side to side. "Show her how, Jeanie."

Jean stretched one leg out behind her and moved into a runner's lunge with the other. Then she raised her arms above her head, palms touching.

"Warrior One!" said Moira. "Now flow it into Warrior Three."

Jean tilted forward, balancing all her weight on one leg and moving the other one straight out behind her. In a slow graceful arc, she reached her arms out to each side. She looked like a figure skater frozen mid-glide.

Moira clapped. "Wonderful! Your turn, Charlotte."

Charlotte held up her hand and backed away.

| Jean and Charlotte had most evenings to themselves. While Jean made dinner, Charlotte wandered through her mother's house, touching familiar pieces of furniture, relics from her childhood, now living in unfamiliar rooms.

She lingered in front of Roger's photo. Twenty years ago, when Charlotte fled to Australia, it wasn't her parents' over-whelming grief that drove her away. Nor was it the knowledge that she could never fill the gap Roger had left in their lives. She could deal with those things. What she couldn't handle was the obliteration of her brother's existence. Their father refused to hold a funeral. He removed every picture of Roger from the house, took down all his trophies from the mantel above the fireplace, and carted all his belongings off to Goodwill.

The silent emptiness in the house had throbbed in Charlotte's head, and her anger pounded at her eardrums. She'd paced their back alley, raging at everyone. At her father for being so hard. At her mother for being so obedient. At her brother for being so dead. When she couldn't stand it any more, she went as far away as she could and still be in an English-speaking country. From then until now, trips back to Canada from Australia were few and brief.

Jean called out that dinner was ready. Charlotte reached out to the photo, touched her brother's face, and went into the kitchen. A newspaper clipping was beside Charlotte's place at the table. Jean still read the city paper every day.

"I cut this out for you. Your high school is having a reunion. This weekend. You should go," said Jean.

"I came here to see you, Mom."

"Yes, I know. But it would do you good to go into the city and see some of your old friends. Like Karen...what was her last name?"

"Watson."

"That's it. Karen Watson. Such a nice girl. Maybe she'll be there."

"I haven't been in touch with Karen for years, Mom."

"Why don't you look her up?"

"Are you trying to get rid of me?"

"Don't be silly. You'd enjoy your vacation more if you didn't have to spend every minute cooped up here."

"That's funny coming from you. I tried everything to get you and Dad out of the house twenty years ago."

"That was different."

They cleared the table and started on the dishes, with Jean washing, Charlotte drying.

"It's good to see that picture of Roger on your wall."

"Yes. It is."

"Do you have more?"

"A few."

"Why did you hide them for so long?"

"They were too upsetting for your father after the accident."

Charlotte hesitated, but they were talking about this for the first time ever, so she decided to press on. "You know it wasn't an accident, Mom."

Jean stopped washing the potato pot and looked at her daughter. "Yes, dear. I know. It was suicide. My son committed suicide."

Charlotte looked away. The word echoed in her ears. Suicide. Silence. Suicide. Silence. Suicide.

"Did you and Dad ever figure out why he did it?"

"Not really. Your father didn't want to talk about it. Only once. It was late, after a nightcap of Scotch." Jean paused, then lowered her voice. "He said that Roger must have had a secret. You know—a closet secret."

For the next few heartbeats, the only sounds in the room were soft clinks as Jean washed cutlery. Charlotte dried the forks, the knives, and placed them in the drawer, making no noise.

"No, Mom. If my brother had a secret, it wasn't that."

"Well, we'll never know for sure, will we?"

"I know for sure. Roger wasn't gay. Dad was wrong. Dad was wrong about a lot of things."

Jean drained the water from the sink and wiped the counter.

"Don't be hard on your father, dear. He's not here to defend himself."

"Why did you let him bully you so much?"

"That's ridiculous. Your father didn't bully me."

"He did so. And you took it. You did everything he said, followed every order. Why?"

"Because on the day we got married, I promised to love, honour, and obey your father. So that's what I did. Let's change the subject. On Friday, you can take my car and go to the reunion. It's only a two-hour drive."

Charlotte threw her dishtowel on the floor. "Give it a rest, Mom. I'm not going to the damn reunion."

| The next morning, after Jean returned from a town council meeting, they went for yet another walk around town. Charlotte knew by now that their strolls culminated in coffee at Moira's café. A flash of purple caftan in the kitchen confirmed Moira's presence. In seconds, she appeared at their table. She pointed across the street to The Perry Pond Café, where a sandwich board sat out front: Soup du Jour: Broccoli Cheddar, Large Bowl, $4.00.

"Blast that Fern Cooper and her helmet-head blue hair. Undercutting my prices. With my recipe!"

"Fern's soup is good, Moira, but yours is better," said Jean.

Moira beamed. "Damn right it is."

She turned to Charlotte. "Enough about soup. I've always been curious about Australia. Tell me more about it. What's a typical day like for you?"

"Well...I go to work. On weekends, I go hiking in the country. I visit my friends."

"A visit! That's what we need. Let's you and I go to Australia," said Moira, poking Jean on the shoulder.

"You know, I've been thinking the same thing," said Jean. "This winter. I've already checked into flights."

Charlotte stiffened. "You have? Air fares are high in winter, Mom."

"That's what pensions are for." Jean laughed as she sipped her coffee.

Afterwards, Charlotte and Jean walked along the beach. The late spring sun had the beginnings of summer heat in it. Charlotte tied her jacket around her waist.

"Now, about that reunion this weekend."

"Not this again, Mom."

"Yes, this again. It will be a good opportunity for you to reconnect with old friends."

"I told you already. I don't have any friends left here. My life is in Brisbane now. That's where my friends are."

They walked on the sand, past the main pier where cottagers brought their boats to fill up with gas.

"January. I think we'll come in January."

Charlotte said nothing for several steps, as she pictured her mother and Moira in her house, meeting Toni.

"It's a long flight, Mom."

"I need to see where you live, Charlotte."

"I live in a plain little house. It's a bit like yours."

"I need to see how you live."

"It's not very exciting. I get up. I go to work. I go out with my friends."

"I want to meet your friends. I want to meet the people you work with. When I think about you, I can't see what's around you. I need to see your life in my mind."

Charlotte stopped walking.

Jean kept moving until she realized her daughter was no longer beside her.

"Charlotte?"

"I work with Toni, Mom."

"Good. I want to meet Tony."

"I live with Toni."

" Then I definitely have to meet him. Why didn't you tell me you were living with someone?"

" Toni is Antonia, Mom. I live with Antonia. She's my partner. At work. At home. In life."

Jean stood still, eyes never leaving Charlotte's face. They were a foot away from each other, the silence separating them broken only by the sound of the lake lapping on the rocks. Charlotte held her mother's gaze for as long as she could. Then she looked down. Jean reached out and raised her daughter's chin up.

" You should have told me, Charlotte. A long time ago."

"I know. I'm sorry."

"I'm coming to Australia in January. With Moira. For a month."

Charlotte nodded.

"And you're going to the reunion. That was your brother's school, too. One of you should be there."

I didn't pay enough attention to the people close to me. I know that now. I thought everyone in my orbit revolved around me. Many people survive that narcissistic period of their lives. I wish I had. I think I could have been a good person.

While watching my life go on without me, I've discovered a few things about futures and pasts that I should've learned before. I should've known the ball was already in my hands. And I dropped it. Even then, I had a chance to pick it up, but I didn't.

It's a scary thing, to examine your own life. To rethink your loyalties, shake out your secrets. Some people, like me, can't do it. Or won't. I probably would have eventually, if I'd given myself the chance. Other people refuse to do it, and keep bluffing their way through life. And others, like Leonard, grit their way through.

Everyone on the team called him "Len-nerd." Emphasis on nerd. He hovered around during our practices and games, lurking on the periphery. It wasn't a menacing lurk. The Nerd was more like a pet.

I didn't think about what else he saw when he pointed his camera at me. I was happy to be his subject, happy to pose. I even felt like I was helping him, holding still for a few extra seconds so he could get good shots. Some were published in the local papers. Those pictures made my dad happy, and the Nerd got a credit in the lower corner, in small letters. Photo by Zawatski.

I'd like to see those pictures again. The Nerd would still have them. I know he would. He preserved our early stories during a time when me and my friends felt like the world was eagerly awaiting our arrival. That's what old photos do—make our early foolish stories last so we can look at them when we're old and remember who we thought we were when we were young. Some of us, like the Nerd, will live to get old—unlike me, who will remain young and foolish forever.

The Viewfinder

Leo Zawatski had always wanted to photograph the wind. For more than twenty years, he'd tried to create the perfect image of its invisible but undeniable presence, its feel on his skin, the way it sounded in his ears when it swelled from gust to gale. He produced good shots, some verging on excellent, but none that completely satisfied him. He'd caught the aftermath of wind: ruined boats on hurricane-pounded shorelines, toppled silos, flattened corn crops littered with shredded barn parts. But he'd never captured that elusive ideal picture depicting the wind in its happening moment.

Once a year, Leo returned to the city of his birth for a short visit. His mother always thanked him for taking time out of his busy, exciting life to spend a few days with "boring old me." Every year she was grateful for, although somewhat puzzled by, the present he brought her, always an impractical token, wrapped in black paper and tied with a white ribbon. This year it was a crystal unicorn he'd found while on a photo assignment in Austria.

On those annual weekend visits, Leo would leave his mother's house on Saturday mornings and take the bus to the city centre. Once there, he'd go for a walk up Main Street and order French fries at the same old diner where his teenaged self would read comic books for hours, escaping the silence of his childhood home.

This time, with his mother working an unexpected inventory shift at Zellers, Leo decided to make his downtown trek on Friday, so he could spend Saturday with her. He'd just left the house when a plastic bag blew down the street, the early morning sun illuminating it from behind. Leo crouched down on one knee and snapped at least twenty shots in rapid succession. He only stopped shooting when the wind died and the bag lay lifeless on the road, a deflated ghost.

Sitting on the bench at the bus stop, Leo brushed flecks of dirt from the knees of his pants and off the sleeves of his brand-new Italian leather jacket. A seasoned traveller who'd visited every continent on the planet, Leo never failed to be astonished that whenever he sat in this particular spot, he felt like a pock-faced teenager again. He could almost feel a zit popping out in the middle of his forehead. This was the self he referred to as the quivering ass, the nerd who timed his weekend bus rides so that he'd be on the same bus as four girls who also went downtown every Saturday morning. They went to the same school he did, were in some of his classes, but never once acknowledged his existence, on or off the bus. That kid was Leonard: the boy who hoped that some day, one of those girls would smile at him.

| Leonard was well aware that he was the class nerd. Every six weeks his father took him to the cheapest barber in town for a buzz cut. His mother bought him short-sleeved plaid polyester shirts on sale at Zellers, the same shirts she bought for his father, only two sizes smaller. Leonard wore his nerdiness with carefully concealed resentment because there wasn't anything else he could do.

For his sixteenth birthday, he received a long yellow scarf and a card signed "from your parents." Four days earlier, his father had received a long green scarf and a card signed "from your wife and son." Eight days later, on Christmas morning, his mother woke him up at precisely eight o'clock, as usual. They shuffled downstairs in their slippers to admire their Christmas tree, Leonard stifling his yawn behind his mother's back.

The Zawatski Christmas tree looked the same from one year to the next. The lights, the shiny white balls, and strings of silver tinsel hung from exactly the same spots on exactly the same green plastic branches. Every year, three presents sat under the tree—the two his mother had bought for her husband and son, and the one she'd bought for them to give to her. She never let father or son do the shopping. She said they wouldn't be practical in their choices.

Every year, the three Christmas presents were wrapped in exactly the same paper, a green and white reindeer pattern on a red background. When Leonard was still a toddler, his mother had found the paper at a Boxing Day sale at Zellers and bought twenty rolls of it. Every year, she tied the same green ribbon around Leonard's present, the same red ribbon around his father's present, and the same white ribbon around her own. She told Leonard that she liked white because it was such an uncomplicated colour.

On the Christmas morning four days after Leonard turned sixteen, he and his mother saw an unusual sight. A fourth present sat in front of the other three, wrapped in black paper and tied with a gold ribbon.

Leonard's mother gasped. "What's this?" she said as she bent down to pick it up.

Leonard, who, until that moment, had wanted only to go back to bed, felt a twinge of curiosity at this Christmas morning irregularity.

"It's quite heavy." Her eyes grew wider as she shook the box. "I wonder who it's for." She flipped open the tag and read out loud. "To Leo. From Dad."

Puzzlement spread across her face. "Leo?"

"For Christ's sake, give it to the boy."

Leonard's father stood fully dressed at the bottom of the stairs, a suitcase on the floor beside him.

"What's going on?" said his mother, looking at the suitcase.

His father took the box out of her hands and shoved it at Leonard. "Open it."

Leonard hesitated, looking at his mother, she still looking at the suitcase.

"Open it right this minute."

Leonard tore into the box. It was a camera, a lightweight compact that came with a long thin strap and a booklet of instructions.

"I had them put three rolls of film in the box. Threw in some extra batteries myself. Now stop hiding in your room. Get out and see the world. Take some pictures while you're at it."

This was the longest string of words the man had uttered to either his wife or his son in sixteen years. With that, he picked up the suitcase and walked to the front door. "Don't wait dinner for me."

And they didn't.

From then on, Leonard became Leo. He never went anywhere without his camera. A few months later, he sold a photograph of a car stuck in a blizzard to the city newspaper. Soon the editor was giving him regular assignments.

His nerdiness was an advantage because his classmates hardly noticed he was there. They were used to having him around. He caught all of them in his lens, including the football team, especially the team captain, Roger Andrews. He captured Coach Bailey shouting instructions from the sidelines,

Roger's father in the background, also shouting. At the end of the school year, he went to the prom and the bush party afterwards, where he took pictures of his classmates' faces lit by the flickering fire.

Leo would never claim that he and Roger had been friends, but they'd had a good camera relationship. Unlike the other players who'd brushed past him, sometimes even pushing him out of the way, Roger had always paused long enough for Leo to get the shots he needed.

The thought of Roger always made Leo's stomach lurch. His death had felt like a physical blow, a tackle from behind. Even now, twenty years later, Leo still couldn't believe it had really happened. One day Roger was so vitally alive. The next day, he wasn't. Dead by choice. Leo had often felt low in his life, but he'd never come close to making that decision. To make Roger's sudden absence even worse, the silence that had immediately swallowed him up made it seem that he'd never lived at all.

Roger's picture never appeared in the community newsletter again. His name disappeared from conversations in the hallways of Victory High. Everyone stopped talking about him. Everyone, except Leo's mother, who asked her son almost every day why that beautiful boy would do such a terrible thing to his family.

Leo spent that the rest of that sad summer picking out his best shots. He put them together in a photo essay called "A Year in the Life of a School," and sent it to his local editor, who sent it to the national head office. The pictures ran in a glossy newsmagazine. They won Leo a scholarship that took him from Victory High to the New York Photography Institute.

In New York City, Leo learned how to see the world through a variety of focal lengths. He learned how to compose strong images, tinker with depths of field, and blur moving subjects by using slow shutter speeds. He learned how to capture the stars as streaks in the night sky by placing his camera on a tripod and holding the aperture open for minutes at a time. Once he started working as a professional photographer, Leo learned how to travel: how to beat jet lag, how to be anonymous anywhere.

| Another plastic bag blew along the street, but the gust was weak and the bag tumbled along the pavement only half-inflated. The bus finally came into sight, a cloud of dust funnelling behind it. As Leo climbed aboard, his mind turned again to those girls, the ones who never gave him a second look when they passed him in the hallways at school, who ignored him as they waited at this bus stop every Saturday morning. He'd always stood aside and boarded after they did. He'd always waited in the aisle until they'd taken their seats, before walking past and choosing one for himself a few rows behind them— not too close, but close enough that he could hear their chatter.

Today, the bus followed its regular route downtown. On the way, it passed Leo's old high school. The main entrance looked the same. Beside the front door was a sign advertising the reunion scheduled for this weekend, starting tonight. Leo had forgotten about it. A few months ago, he'd received a letter from Coach Bailey, now the principal, telling him about the reunion and asking for permission to display the photo essay he'd done during his senior year. When Leo consented, Principal Bailey had sent him a complimentary reunion pass, which Leo threw in the recycling bin.

From his seat on the bus, Leo saw two white tents, one larger than the other, set up at the end of the football field. He knew the bigger one had to be a beer tent—it wouldn't be a reunion without a beer tent. Leo enjoyed beer now. He'd avoided the sudsy beverage back in high school, afraid it would make him do something stupid.

As the bus stopped for a red light, Leo watched a catering truck pull up to the big tent. Maybe he'd go after all. Just for a beer. It might be a welcome diversion to check out the scene and watch people react to his old pictures. Above the tents, he saw green and gold balloons floating, tugging gently on the strings tethering them to the main poles. He'd take his camera. Perhaps the wind would pick up.

What happens when you're not around to own your future?
What happens to your future when you're not part of it anymore?
I didn't think about those questions that night. But I've had time
to think since then. Your future happens whether you're in it
or not.

How do I talk about Lisa? I've never talked about her to
anyone. Together, we were a force out of sync, misaligned in time.

She didn't look like a teacher when she approached me in the
gym one day and said she knew my sister. I helped her carry bags
of volleyballs out to the team bus. Sometimes she watched our
football practices and games. After the concussion, she offered me
some training tips. One night, when it was raining hard, I saw her
standing at the bus stop. I drove her home in my van. That van
became our hideaway.

I danced with her just one time. That night. Graduation night.
At the dance. In the gym where we met.

I saw her eyes that night at the bush party, the crescent moon
reflected in them like curved lightsabres. I remember the two
words she whispered into my ear, so softly I almost didn't hear
them. I didn't have to. I knew what they were. And I knew I wasn't
a good person.

I abandoned her that night. Walked away. When I did that,
I abandoned myself.

I didn't have a fraction of her courage.

All aftermaths have a before. All futures have a past. And the
future begins in the past, long before the aftermath. But the after-
math isn't inevitable. It can be altered. Maybe that's why I'm
stuck here. To alter the aftermath.

Willpower

The first time Victory High School hired Lisa Martin, she was just out of university, twenty-three years old, humming with ambition, sure of herself and her knowledge, unaware that she didn't know anything yet. She was thrilled to get her first teaching job and be assigned a Phys Ed class right away. Some of her students were only five years younger than she was.

Shortly after the school year started, Lisa ran into a friend from university, Charlotte Andrews. "You're teaching at my old high school. My kid brother still goes there. Look around for him. He's cool."

So Lisa met Roger. She still didn't quite understand the power of the feelings that engulfed them. The whole thing was her fault. She should have stopped it. But her body felt as if some alien force had taken control. Then she made it worse. She should have simply disappeared without telling him. What possessed her to show up at the bush party after the prom? She felt what she saw in his eyes, wide and white as he backed away from her. Panic renders rational minds irrational.

A week later, she resigned from her job. That night she told her father about her situation. Her mother had died eight years earlier and Lisa had never missed her more than she did that night. Her father pulled a wad of cash from his pocket. This didn't surprise Lisa. She knew he always felt more secure when he had at least ten fifty-dollar bills on him. He handed her the entire roll.

"Your mother would be very disappointed in you."

The next day she bought herself a used car and drove east to a city two provinces away. In the fall, she found a temporary teaching job that lasted until the last few weeks of her pregnancy.

| Lisa's infant son grew into a healthy toddler. She was surprised when it became evident that he was left-handed. Nobody in her family was left-handed. She tried putting the toys he played with into his right hand, but he always shifted them to his left, a display of individuality she found endearing. In fact, everything about her boy enchanted her. Inevitably, her active and curious son started school. That's when he also started asking questions. The one she dreaded came on a Sunday morning. All the other kids had fathers. Why didn't he? She said that his father had gone away and could never come back. After that, Lisa decided that Will should know at least one member of his extended family. She had no siblings. Only her father, who still lived alone on his farm. Will was nine years old when they moved back to her hometown.

Teaching jobs were few that fall. She had one offer—her old job at Victory High, vacated abruptly because of illness. Lisa was hesitant, but during the years she'd been away, the school had undergone a complete turnover of staff. Almost. The only teacher who remained from Lisa's time there was Jim Bailey. Back then, he'd been the football coach. Now he was the principal. Lisa accepted the job and bought a small house in another neighbourhood so that Will would go to a different school.

| If John Martin was happy to have his daughter back, he didn't show it. But he and Will formed an immediate bond. One night several months after their return, after Will had gone to bed, John arrived on Lisa's doorstep and demanded to know the name of his grandson's father. "I have a right to know."

"No, you don't," said Lisa.

"Will has a right to know."

"What about my rights?"

Lisa's father never asked about his grandson's paternity again. On Sundays, Lisa dropped Will off at the farm. She knew they'd spend all afternoon in the workshop next to the barn, restoring John's old motorcycle. For dinner, they'd have burgers at Rose's Café before John dropped Will off at home.

As Will approached his sixteenth birthday, all he could talk about was getting his driver's license. Lisa was less than thrilled about the prospect of Will at the wheel. She wanted him to wait, at least until winter was over. But Will was insistent. They argued about it almost every day. One Sunday night, when her father dropped Will off, he stood at his daughter's front door and asked to have a word. She stepped outside.

"The boy's ready to drive. You're holding him back."

"He's my son, not yours."

"He'll be a fine driver. Stop acting like a scared ninny. You'll turn him into a Mama's boy."

"Good night, Dad," she said as she closed the door.

To Lisa's dismay, Will passed his driver's test on the first try. He asked to borrow Lisa's car that very night.

"I'm sorry, Will. You're not insured, and I can't afford to add you to the policy right now."

The next Sunday, Will came home with a cheque from his grandfather to cover his insurance.

For the next several months, mother and son engaged in a verbal tug-of-war. Will would ask to use the car, and Lisa would say no: she needed it, or it was low on gas, or it had to go in for an oil change, or the roads were too wet, or it was too windy. Will didn't give up.

"Why don't you stay home? I'll drive out to Granddad's. You can have the afternoon to yourself."

Lisa checked the sky. "The weather looks a little iffy. Like there's snow in the air. The roads could get icy. I'll drive."

Will slouched in the passenger seat, his arms across his chest. When they arrived at John's place, Will got out and slammed the car door.

"Stop it, Will. You're acting like a six-year-old."

"Why won't you let me drive?"

"After the stunt you pulled last weekend? No way."

"I just took the car to the store to get some snacks."

"Without my permission."

"You were asleep. I didn't want to wake you up. I'm a licensed driver now."

"Just because you have your license doesn't mean you know how to drive."

Lisa covered her mouth with her hand, shocked to hear her father's decades-old words coming out in her voice. She saw the look on her son's face.

"You're going to be a good driver, Will."

"How would you know? You don't trust me enough to give me a chance."

"It's not you. It's everyone else I don't trust."

"If I had a dad, he'd let me drive."

That night, Lisa and Will came to an agreement: he could drive the car in the evenings, but not after midnight.

| John Martin met his neighbours for breakfast at Rose's Café three times a week. His favourite topic was his grandson. "Almost eighteen now. Smart as a firecracker. Still growing. I swear that kid's going to be seven feet tall."

One morning, John bragged to his friends about how easily Will handled the old Harley they'd worked on together. " The boy took to it like a duck. . ."

John's sentence went forever unfinished. He collapsed face down on the table. At the hospital, the doctor told Lisa that her father had suffered a brain aneurysm. "Even if an ambulance had been waiting right outside the restaurant, they couldn't have saved him."

The week after her father's funeral, Lisa and Will went to the farm to clean out John's belongings. They were quiet on the drive, quiet as she parked in front of the house, quiet as they walked up the steps.

Their footsteps echoed as they walked through the small rooms. John had lived alone for a long time and the house had a distinctively old-man feel. Everything was a shade of brown— the carpets were dark brown, the furniture was medium brown, and the lampshades were light brown.

For most of that morning, Lisa and Will worked in silence as they packed up John's personal items. She'd brought ten boxes with her, but soon realized they wouldn't need that many. Her father didn't have much—a meagre wardrobe, a dozen or so books, a few photographs. A sepia photo of Lisa's mother and a school picture of Will sat next to each other on the nightstand beside his bed. She was surprised to see a photo of herself at about the same age Will was now sitting between the other two.

Finished, they took one last look around the house. Will shook his head.

"One tiny television. No computer. How could Granddad have lived like this for so long?"

" This was his life. It's all he wanted."

"I think he wanted more. He told me he wished he'd gone to Ireland to see where his mother was born."

"I never knew that."

"Maybe you should've asked him."

"Probably. It was hard for Dad and me to talk. We never did get along, especially after Mom died."

"At least you had a dad."

Lisa took a deep breath.

"I know it's been hard for you, Will. But I did the best I could. What would a father have done that I haven't?"

"He'd tell me his name."

Lisa opened her mouth to speak, but nothing came out. She watched Will cross the yard toward the barn. She finished packing up the car, and went to find him in the workshop, sitting on the motorcycle. He smiled at her. Will never stayed angry for long.

"It must have been fun growing up on a farm. Driving tractors, playing in the loft."

Lisa shook her head. "I never drove a tractor and I wasn't allowed in the loft."

"Why not?"

"I'm a girl. Every time I came out here, Dad sent me back to the house to help Mom. I was happy to get away from this place and go to university."

"What are you going to do with the motorcycle?"

"Sell it, I guess."

"Can I have it?"

"Absolutely not. Motorcycles are dangerous."

"Granddad said he was going to give it to me."

"He should have talked to me first."

Will roared the motorcycle engine to life and took off out
the shed door, raising dust as he sped down the long driveway.
Lisa watched him disappear down the road.

She wandered around the shop, picking up her father's tools
and opening the drawers under the workbench. In the corner,
his coveralls hung from a hook. She gathered them in her hands
and buried her nose in the faded denim, inhaling deeply. A hint
of Zest soap lurked under the smell of oil.

Lisa sat on the bench outside the barn until Will returned.
He put the motorcycle back in the shed and walked to the
passenger side of the car. His mother threw him the keys.

"I'm tired. You drive."

| Lisa paced back and forth across the staff lounge. Her teaching
duties done for the day, it would be at least an hour before Will
picked her up. These days, he seemed to think her car was his.
Every weekday morning, he dropped her off at school, drove all
the way across town to his university campus, and returned to
get her in the afternoon.

With the school year winding down, the week had already
been a strenuous one. Today, she'd refereed the final games in
her intramural basketball league in the morning, taught two
Phys Ed classes in the afternoon, and spent her lunch break
marking the tests her history class handed in yesterday. She
checked her watch again: only two minutes had passed. She
pulled on her sweater and headed for the door.

Outside the school's main entrance, she inhaled the fresh
afternoon air and rubbed her temples as she walked. The dull
ache across the base of her skull began to ease.

Her feet took her toward the football field. On the track encircling the field, a group of runners dashed past her. She shivered a little and threw her sweater around her shoulders, but she wasn't cold. Lisa usually went out of her way to avoid this side of the school. Ten years had passed since her return to Victory High. Last summer, she had finally made herself come out here, sit up in that grandstand, and face the empty field that still looked the same as it had twenty years earlier.

The pack of runners caught up to her again. Lisa stood aside to let them pass and saw her car pull up in front of the school. She also saw Jim Bailey come out of the school and head in Will's direction. When Will started walking toward Jim, Lisa broke into a run. She was out of breath when she reached them.

"Ah, Lisa," said Jim. "I've been looking for you. We need a referee for the old-timers' volleyball game that kicks off the reunion tomorrow. We've got a net set up in the hockey rink beside the beer tent."

Lisa had avoided having anything to do with the reunion. "I don't think so, Jim. Will and I might catch a movie together tomorrow night."

"Can't. I've got a date."

"A date?"

"Yes. With Laura."

"Laura?"

Will grinned at her. "The girl from the bakery. We got to talking last week when I picked up your granola."

"And you're taking her out for dinner?"

"Yes, Mom.

"Isn't that a bit fast? Shouldn't you go for coffee first instead of a full-blown dinner?"

"Mom. We've already been out for a few runs together. Now I'm taking her out for dinner. But we can pick you up here afterwards."

"No," said Lisa, louder than she meant to. "I'll get a ride home with someone else."

"Excellent," said Jim, rubbing his hands together. "We're all set."

Lisa stood in silence as she listened to the two of them talk football. She studied Jim's face closely, holding her breath as she waited for Victory High's former football coach to see what she did every time she looked at her son. When Jim's expression didn't change, Lisa allowed herself to breathe again.

Saying that I didn't mean to hurt anyone only makes it worse. Intentions, like life, must be examined. Honestly. No lying to yourself. No protecting yourself. Myself.

I thought I was born lucky. I had so much luck that I expected it to be with me always. I grew reckless and careless. I hurt people—people at the centre of my life, people I took for granted, people who needed more from me, not less.

My limbo has forced me to witness the consequences of what I did, consequences that are still unravelling. This reunion is a magnet for them. Mom. Char. Leo. Keith. Lisa. Will. All converging in the eye of my hurricane.

And now the girls. Only three left. Four minus one.

They drove me nuts. Always giggling. Always together, as if invisible strings connected them through their hipbones.

Amy was okay. I used to think she'd be less annoying if she'd had different friends. Maggie was a bubble on the verge of bursting. Exhausting.

The whole team let loose on Val. Poor slutty Val. They passed her around like a toy. A toy I didn't want to play with. She made me want to run the other way.

All the guys wanted a piece of Kerrie-Lynn. They were careful what they said in front of her twin brother Keith. Not that it mattered. She'd have nothing to do with any of them. But I had a feeling she'd say yes to me. I was right. And ashamed afterwards. She was golden, and I used her. My plan was to brag. But I couldn't.

The Dead List

Despite her claustrophobia, Amy Crawford liked flying. She always booked a window seat, for the feeling of space and the view. But she'd made a mistake today—she was right over the wing. Amy strained against her seatbelt, her forehead almost touching the window glass as she looked backward and forward across the wing's expanse, eyes scanning the prairie grid far below. Finally, she felt the plane's speed cut back and soon she saw the outskirts of the city she'd grown up in, the one she hadn't visited for twenty years. As the ground came closer, she scanned the skyline, but couldn't see anything she recognized. Her hometown looked alien.

In a hotel room down the block from her former high school, Amy changed her clothes and unpacked her weekend wardrobe. This hotel was new, at least to her, built sometime in the last two decades. On the website, it had looked stylish and modern. In reality, it was unremarkable: tired, with a weird smell. Was it the lingering scent of a strong cleanser or pungent disinfectant used to cover up something rotting in an unseen crevice? She stepped out onto the balcony and surveyed her old neighbourhood.

At eighteen, she'd been restless. Real life happened elsewhere, to other people. She felt like a permanent spectator, and wanted to be a participant. A summer job at a mountain resort out west was irresistible. She left right after graduation and never came back. Until today. With her thirty-eighth birthday looming, Amy felt an unusual yearning for the old days.

She finished unpacking, hanging her clothes with all the hanger hooks facing the same way on the rod. In the bathroom mirror, she examined her reflection. *How do I look compared to twenty years ago? Will they recognize me?*

Amy checked her watch. Only four-thirty. An hour and a half until the opening reception in the beer tent, where she'd arranged to meet Val and Maggie. She opened the book she'd brought in case the reunion turned out to be a total bore. She read three lines and closed it again, unable to concentrate.

The early June air was warm as Amy stood on the football field, looking from one goalpost to the other. Beyond the end zone was a huge white tent. Above it stretched an enormous banner: Victory High School Celebrates 25 Amazing Years!

Amy walked through the end zone to the tent. A hot-dog stand was not yet operating, its attendant searching for a source of electricity. A volleyball net set up inside the boards of the hockey rink looked incongruous. Two teams of alumni laughed their way through a game. Many players had flabby bellies under their team shirts. Several wore knee braces, others elbow pads—a few had both. Amy thought she recognized Dina Spinetti, but wasn't sure. She did recognize Miss Martin refereeing the game, and was surprised she was still teaching at Victory High twenty years later.

What looked like one huge tent turned out to be two. The biggest was the beer tent, at the moment almost empty. Two volunteers set up a table for drink tickets, while another organized a souvenir stand. In the smaller tent, two people struggled to hang a display of photographs.

Scarves, pennants, old school jackets, and pom-pom shakers adorned every post. And beanie hats. Those stupid beanie hats Amy had always despised floated down from the roof every two or three feet, each one hanging on a length of fishing line. She had often been the only student in the grandstands not wearing a beanie hat. She'd never understood why people insisted on making themselves look ridiculous.

One of the volunteers smiled at Amy and said the bar wasn't open yet.

"That's okay. I can wait," Amy replied, trying to picture how the tent would look in a few hours. "How many people are you expecting tonight?"

"It's going to be packed. It's not just a regular reunion for one graduating year. This one is special. It's for everyone who ever went to Victory High."

Amy went back outside. She watched the volleyball game for a few moments. When Miss Martin glanced in her direction, Amy turned away. With still no sign of Val or Maggie, she decided to walk around the block. One block turned into two, then three. At street level, her hometown felt unchanged, as if she'd travelled back in time. Even the cracks in the sidewalks looked the same as they had when she'd skipped the three blocks to her elementary school. *Step on a crack, break your mother's back.* On good days, she made sure she jumped over cracks; on bad days, she stomped on them.

Amy wandered back to the football field and clambered up the old grandstand. It creaked under her weight just as it had twenty years ago. From the top tier, the view was exactly the same as it had always been. She and Val liked to watch the games from way up here, because the high vantage point allowed them to keep an eye on the field action, the bench, and the cheerleading squad, led by Maggie and Kerrie-Lynn.

Kerrie-Lynn. Even after all these years, Amy still couldn't believe that her friend was dead. She had to be in this world, living a life somewhere.

Amy didn't enjoy sports, didn't like the feeling that she might lose control of her body, her composure, her emotions. For her, going fast, whether by car or boat, on skis or on foot, was an uncomfortable experience. Her favourite activity was hiking, where she maintained control over her own measured steps.

Watching sports wasn't much better. As a spectator, Amy was impatient for whatever game she was watching to end. She particularly disliked fast games like basketball and hockey. They blurred in front of her eyes.

Football was different. The game had time between plays that made a lot of sense to Amy. That was the part she'd liked to watch, the part where the players went into a huddle, that tight circle where they put their heads together to make a plan. Once the ball was in motion, she usually closed her eyes.

Amy's friends knew she thought football was tedious. She told them she went to the games to be with them. She didn't tell them that she also went to watch Roger. Today, back up in these grandstands, she squeezed her eyes shut to dispel his image, and pictured her friends instead.

Amy, Val, Maggie, and Kerrie-Lynn had been an inseparable quartet from their earliest days in elementary school. Their homes were mere blocks apart. Even their birthdays were all on the same day—different months of course—but all on the ninth day. They'd felt like sisters by choice rather than birth.

Every Saturday morning, the four friends had taken a bus downtown, where they spent the day hanging out at their favourite department store, the one with the restaurant designed like a steamship. At the entrance was a large paddle wheel that rotated over a shallow pond littered with pennies,

nickels, and dimes, but never any quarters. *Was it still there?*
Maybe she'd go downtown tomorrow. Maybe Val and Maggie
would want to come, although it would feel strange to make
that trip without Kerrie-Lynn.

"Amy! Is that you up there?"

| Val Repko was certain they'd agreed to meet at five-thirty in
front of the beer tent, but when she arrived, the familiar faces
she expected to see were nowhere. Not at the hot-dog stand,
or the popcorn machine, or the tedious old-timers' volleyball game. Was that Beth Skinner still spiking the ball at centre?
Val went inside the beer tent and searched through the sparse
crowd. She checked the smaller tent, where the photography
displays waited for an audience. It was empty.

She was sure she'd recognize her two friends as soon as she
saw them. In their online messages, they both said that they
hadn't deteriorated too badly. It was odd that they hadn't asked
each other for pictures. Everybody posted pictures online
these days. But Amy and Maggie didn't mention an exchange
of photos, so Val didn't either. Maybe they'd gotten fat. Not
likely. People who'd let themselves get fat probably didn't go to
their high-school reunions. Val had searched for her friends on
Facebook, but apparently they were resisting social media. Val
knew that wasn't out of character for Amy, but not Maggie, who
had to be included in everything.

As for her own appearance, Val figured she looked much the
same as she had back then, apart from her dyed red hair and her
new breasts. Amy and Maggie were certain to notice them. Val
had picked out her "girls" with Kerrie-Lynn's knockout set
in mind.

Kerrie-Lynn. Val would never forget the day she'd heard, about a year after they graduated. After the catastrophe of grad night, the four friends, like most of their class, had scattered across the continent, so the news had circulated slowly. Val found a short obituary that offered no clues as to what had happened. She'd called Maggie first, then Amy, both as shocked, upset, and puzzled as she was. She'd tried to call Kerrie-Lynn's twin brother Keith, but he seemed to have vanished. When she phoned their older sister Karen, all she got was an answering machine. Val left a message, but no one ever responded.

Various rumours made the rounds. One was that it had been a hit-and-run accident. Another claimed it was a kidnapping gone bad. Yet another theory was that Kerrie-Lynn had been murdered while walking through east Los Angeles by herself late at night. That was absurd. Kerrie-Lynn was too smart to walk through a dangerous area alone.

Kerrie-Lynn should have been the most successful of them all. She should have been a star, or running a talent agency, or the head of a movie production company by now. Even as a teenager, she'd had a magnetic aura. Every boy at school had asked her out, but Kerrie-Lynn maintained she didn't want a boyfriend, and always said no.

Val never said no.

Val couldn't get away from her hometown fast enough. Hardly pausing long enough to say goodbye to her family, she left town on a red-eye flight and never came back. Fortunately for Val, her parents liked visiting Toronto. She'd done well in the last two decades. Her career in banking was solid, providing her not only with a high income, but also a regular supply of men, men she could entertain herself with and cut off as soon as they no longer interested her.

The beer tent was filling up now. Val searched the faces. Some looked familiar, but she couldn't put names to any of them. She recognized one man standing alone in the middle of the tent. She was certain he used to be that nerdy kid in her Physics class, the one who always had a camera hanging around his neck. She noticed his elegant leather jacket. Probably Italian. Back in school, he had worn nerdy plaid shirts and the same jeans every day. But it had to be him, the kid from the bus. The camera slung over his shoulder convinced her she was right. *What was his name?*

He looked in her direction. Val turned away. *Damn. Why can't I remember his name?* She decided it was silly not to be friendly, so she waved. He smiled and took her picture. She made a fast exit toward the football field.

Walking past the uprights, Val could almost hear the roars that used to follow every touchdown. Every game, as she and Amy sat up in the grandstand, Val had a hard time sitting still. Her feet wanted to run, and her hands always went up to make the catch. She would much rather have been playing than watching. She never said this out loud to anyone.

Instead, Val learned how it felt to play the game from the players. As they took her clothes off, she would make them tell their game stories. It didn't take much to get them talking, especially about themselves. As soon as one guy's stories got boring, she'd move on to the next one. For a while, she liked the placekicker because he talked about teeing the ball up at exactly the right angle for his foot to make perfect contact. Then she worked her way through the receivers. They had the most exciting stories to tell, about near misses that slipped out of their grasp, or the ones they managed to hang on to even as the opposing team pulled them down. She didn't like the line-backers: they had no necks and didn't want to talk at all.

Val went through the whole team. On her terms, not theirs. Her only failure was the quarterback. Roger had always resisted her advances, even on grad night.

Grad night. Val looked around for the nearest distraction, and saw the lone figure sitting up on the grandstand. Amy jumped up when Val shouted at her. "Don't come down. I'll come up."

They met in the middle, hugging and saying "You Look Amazing" at exactly the same moment.

"No, really, you look great," said Val.

"Not fat?"

"No way. Skinny as a rail. How about me? Notice anything different?"

"Well, it has been twenty years but let's see…you always changed your hair colour every other week, so the red is not really a surprise. And you're not wearing glasses yet. Nope, you look pretty much the same. I'd have known you anywhere. Wait! I know—you pierced more holes in your ears."

"Never mind."

"Any sign of Maggie yet?"

"No. I didn't want to be the first one in the beer tent, so I came up here. Remember how we used to watch from up top? Wasn't that great? Oh, Val. Let's talk. Tell me about your job. Did you finally pick one guy? Any kids? Gosh, there's so much to catch up on."

Val laughed at Amy's rush of words. "You're probably the only person left in the world who still uses the word 'gosh.' Fuck no, I didn't pick one guy. And no, no, no to kids. My job's fine. It pays the bills and lets me take two holidays every year.

Ever been to the Cook Islands? You've just got to go. They have the hottest..."

"Look!" Amy pointed out onto the field.

Val turned in time to see a matronly woman throw herself into a cartwheel about twenty yards ahead of them. The move fell apart halfway through, and the would-be acrobat collapsed into a heap.

| *Damn*. Maggie Morris had been sure she could still do those cartwheels. When she was a cheerleader, she could do three in a row and still jump up higher than anyone else for the big finish. She tried to haul herself off the ground, but fell back and closed her eyes.

She was tired. She'd used points to book her flight, which meant that she'd left for the airport at four this morning, and that her plane had made two stops along the way, turning what was normally a three-hour direct flight into an eight-hour marathon. *I wonder if I look as dumpy as I feel. If I look like I've had three kids.*

For six months, Maggie had given up her daily Starbucks latte and steered some cash away from household funds so she could make this trip. She'd spent the last week cooking extra meals, doing the laundry, and enlisting her neighbours to be on standby. She knew that by having everything well organized on the home front before she left, she'd have an easier time coaxing Bud out of his anger when she got back.

Maggie loved being a mom, but she was restless. The last twenty years of her life felt like they'd evaporated, vanished with the wind. Bud wanted her home with the kids, didn't want her to get a job. After high school, she'd been excited to move out west. Back then, she'd thought The Red Dot would be an upper-class place to work. But it turned out to be a burger joint with a liquor licence and a bartender named Bud. *I shouldn't be so hard on Bud. At heart, he's a good man.*

She opened her eyes. The sky wavered, blue beyond blue beyond blue, undulations to infinity. Her eyelids closed again. Back in high school, anything had seemed possible. Now, nothing did. Something had gone wrong inside her, but she couldn't locate the cause of her. . .her what? Her pain? She couldn't call it pain. It was more like discomfort. A throb in her lungs. A gnawing in her gut. No, that sounded too much like cramps. It was a gap. No. Deeper than that: more than malaise, less than rage.

Maggie's eyes opened to see Amy and Val hovering over her. "Are you all right?" They pulled her up to a sitting position. "Stay there. Don't get up too fast."

"I'm okay."

They pulled her to her feet and Maggie brushed grass from her butt. Amy and Val enveloped her in a hug. Then they all stood back.

Damn, damn, damn. They both look great. I should have gone shopping. I should have done my nails. I should have had liposuction.

"Maggie, you look just the same. I'd have known you anywhere," said Amy.

"Gosh, really?"

Amy and Val burst out laughing. Maggie didn't understand why, but not understanding was a familiar feeling. Back in high school, she'd often felt left out of the easy communication between her three best friends. She remembered laughing just because the others were laughing, laughing even if she didn't get the joke. She knew she wasn't as smart as her friends. To compensate for her lack of witty verbal skills, Maggie trained herself to notice unspoken details. She saw how people held themselves, paid more attention to what they did than what they said.

Amy looked the same as high-school Amy. Val looked different.

"Val, when did you get those breasts?"

"That's it!" laughed Amy. "Come on, 'fess up."

"I haven't the faintest idea what you're talking about," said Val with a sly grin.

"Wow," said Maggie. "Here we are. On the football field. After all this time. It feels weird."

And there he was. *Roger.* In her head. *Geez, Roger. Would she ever be able to shake the feeling that she should have known?* She'd lived next door to the Andrews family. Roger was the sunny kid she used to play with in the back lane. He could climb any tree. And he did: climbed them all. The day before they graduated, Roger had appeared in her yard. She gestured for him to sit on the steps beside her, but he wanted to stand. He was all motion that day, shifting from foot to foot, doing his funny fist-pounding thing. He always pounded his right fist into his left hand while he talked. That day, the fist-pounding was intense, and he almost seemed to forget she was there. Finally, she started to pound her own hand into her fist in imitation. He realized what she was doing, laughed it off, and sauntered away. *See you tomorrow, Mags.*

"Look at them all," said Amy, gesturing to people streaming toward the beer tent.

"Shall we join them?" said Val.

"I'm not quite ready to share you two with everyone else yet," said Maggie.

"It is a little early to start drinking," said Amy. "Maggie, are you sure you're all right? You look a bit pale."

"Don't worry about me," said Maggie. "Let's check out the school before we go to the tent. We can find the registration table and pick up our packages."

| They all remembered the school as a huge structure with daunting grey concrete walls. Now, the once-imposing entrance felt small and trivial, like the doorway to an old strip mall. Inside, halls that had often been passages to humiliation and punishment were ordinary institutional corridors.

Standing in the line at the registration desk outside the cafeteria felt natural, as if they were once again waiting for one of those bad lunches. Soon all three had their name badges pinned onto their shirts. Val and Maggie put on their complimentary souvenir beanies.

"Not in this lifetime," said Amy, stuffing hers into the nearest garbage can.

A cluster of people milled around a large bulletin board covered with pictures and information about reunion activities. A small crowd stood in front of a single page posted below a small wreath and a sign that read "We'll miss you forever."

"What's this?" asked Amy of no one in particular.

"The dead list."

All three friends wanted to walk away. All three knew they couldn't. They stood back and waited until the crowd had dispersed. When a gap opened up between them and the list, they moved in closer. Their eyes fell on the name at the top. They knew who it would be.

Roger had been everybody's friend and nobody's enemy. Every girl in their class had wanted to date him. Every girl's mother had wanted her daughter to date him. Amy, Maggie, and Val suspected that even Kerrie-Lynn would have gone out with Roger had he asked her. But he hadn't dated anyone, and managed to do this without hurting anybody's feelings.

With his lanky body, mop of blond hair, and vivid blue eyes, Roger was a standout in any crowd. People were drawn to him because he saw the upside of every situation. He never missed a party, and never failed an exam. In their senior year, Roger had run for class president. No one ran against him. Teachers and coaches nominated him for all the top academic and sports awards. Adults noted that he was courteous to his mother, nice to his sister, and respectful to his father. Living next door to him, Maggie saw more than others did. She noticed that he was always a little quieter when his father was around. But then again, most teenagers were quiet around fathers, especially their own.

As graduation approached, Val had spent weeks trying to convince Roger that the class president had to have a date for the prom. She had an inkling that Kerrie-Lynn had also asked Roger to take her to the prom, because she'd seen them walking home from school together a few times. In the end, they'd all gone together, on one big date, four girls and three guys crowded into a white limousine.

Amy, Maggie, and Val stood motionless in front of that horrible list, each one thinking of grad night. The formalities had included dinner and dancing in the gym, which had been all decked out in a lush tropical theme. An official photographer posed the graduates beside a fake palm tree. No one had to be urged to smile for the constant camera flashes. No one started a food fight during dinner. No one was left holding up the wall during the dancing.

Then came the bush party. The new Victory High graduates gathered at their favourite hangout by the murky brown waters of the river. A stone-ringed pit contained ashes accumulated from many bonfire nights away from prying parents' eyes. Their class hadn't been into drugs. A few students had joints of marijuana in their pockets that night, but the high of choice came from an aluminum can or a small flask. Music blared from battery-powered boomboxes. The bonfire burned high into the sky as couples drifted into the shadowy bushes. In the beginning, the friends stayed together at the bonfire, roasting hot dogs on long crooked sticks, watching everyone else come and go.

Midnight became the middle of the night. Those around the fire noticed Roger standing off to one side in an intense conversation with the school's new Phys Ed teacher. Maggie thought it was strange that she was there. No other teachers had come to the party, not even Coach Bailey. Roger disappeared into the bushes after Miss Martin left. When he re-emerged, Kerrie-Lynn went to talk to him. Their heads bent together, foreheads almost touching for a moment. Then Roger pulled away from her, backed into the dark shrubbery, and Kerrie-Lynn left, without saying goodbye to anyone. To Amy and Maggie, that wasn't unusual. Kerrie-Lynn could sometimes be a bit moody.

When he reappeared a while later, Roger sank down beside the bonfire, rubbing the back of his neck. Keith asked if he was okay, and Roger nodded. That was when Val took two more beers from the cooler, and pulled Roger away from the group. The next time anyone saw him was at about three in the morning, an inebriated Val leading him toward his van. Roger seemed a little unsteady on his feet. This made the friends giggle because Roger wasn't much of a drinker. He was usually the designated driver. But it was grad night—even Roger was allowed to get drunk.

A while later, Val emerged from the van. When Roger didn't appear, they all figured he was sleeping it off. Keith said he'd hang around and make certain the fire was out. Maggie and Amy walked Val home. It took an hour, but the night was warm.

A security guard found Roger's van in the morning. It hadn't moved. The exhaust pipe had been redirected into the vehicle with a flexible dryer vent, secured in place with duct tape. The vehicle was sealed up like a Christmas box ready to be mailed. Even the windows were taped shut. The keys were still in the ignition, in the on-position. The gas tank was empty. Roger was still in the back.

When the police confronted Val, she became hysterical. She said she couldn't remember anything about the bush party, didn't remember going into the van, didn't remember coming out.

After a brief investigation, the police ruled Roger's death a suicide. No obituary appeared in the local newspaper. Over the next week, Victory High's students cleared out their lockers. Teachers finished their year-end marking. Roger's picture as class president disappeared from the school foyer and an awkward silence shrouded the halls. Roger went from being the most prominent student in the school to a name whispered only in corners.

Val moved away the following week. On the way to the airport, her taxi passed under the train bridge, decorated with new graffiti, carved out in artful eight-foot high letters: *Roger, We'll Never Forget You. Val—Bitch, Slut, Whore.*

Standing in front of the dead list, Amy, Val, and Maggie didn't move, didn't even seem to be breathing. At the bottom of the list, a name had been crossed off with several hand-drawn pen strokes. Leonard Zawatski. Amy pointed to his name.

"Look! That's Leonard. You know, Len-*nerd*."

"That's who it was," said Val with a slap to her forehead. "He's here. I saw him earlier in the beer tent, still holding a camera in his hands."

"Can you imagine finding your own name on a dead list?"

They all laughed. It felt good to laugh.

"And what if you didn't have a pen to cross it off with? I'd start shouting—quick, someone get me a pen so I can bring myself back to life!"

Just above Leonard's crossed-off name was another name, one that hadn't been crossed off and brought back to life. *Kerrie-Lynn Watson.* Date of death was the ninth of July, her birthday, nineteen years ago, just one year after they'd all graduated from high school.

Maggie reached out and touched Kerrie-Lynn's name with her fingertips.

"What happened to you?"

I didn't hate football. But I didn't love it, either. I was good at it. But just because you're good at something doesn't mean you have to do it. I figured I could be good at a lot of things. Like climbing mountains. Or flying planes. Or fighting fires. I tried to tell Dad that I wasn't sure I wanted to play pro ball. And he always came back with the story of his truncated football career. That he knew he'd had what it took, even if he was left-handed. What he lacked was a father to encourage him. It would be a waste to squander my talent.

Coach used to tell me I had luck in my hands. I liked hearing that, liked having hands instilled with luck. It felt like lightning. My fingers tingled as I gripped the ball, looking for a receiver.

Sometimes good luck goes missing for a while, leaving room for bad luck to take over. Mine always came back. Dad used to say there was no such thing as luck. All I needed was grit. Lots of people told me that's what made me a good quarterback—grit. As it turned out, I didn't have enough. I needed another whole truckload.

Coach had been my chance. All that winter and spring, he'd ask how I was. Once he saw me rubbing the back of my neck at my locker.

"You sure you're okay, Ace?"

"Right as rain, Coach." I lied to him. I lied to everyone, including myself. Now I have to watch the carnival I created blow up.

It's done now. Stand strong, Lisa. Be kind, Will. Hug Mom for me, Char. Know that I'm sorry.

I'll watch as long as I can, until the dissipation sets in. Until my dissolve is complete. Until I melt into the ether.

The Beer Tent

The scene looked as if a small circus, minus the animals, had taken up residence in the football field's end zone. Green and gold balloons floated above the two white tents, the smaller one set slightly behind the bigger one. The parking lot filled to capacity, then overflowed onto the grass. People surged through the gate under the long white banner, then stopped at a booth to buy beer and drink tickets. Some walked away with perforated ticket strings as long as their arms.

Between the entrance and the two tents were the food vendors. What went best with beer? Pizza slices the size of a frying pan or jumbo frankfurters? Popcorn from the giant popper or soft doughy pretzels? Inside the glass of a yellow cart, the salty treats dangled on rotating spindles. Sweet savoury aromas mingled in the air. Speakers mounted on tall black stands throbbed with the sounds of "Takin' Care of Business" and "Dancing in the Streets." Above the music, a squeal rang out: "Janie! Janie Anderson! Is that really you?" The answer came back in an instant: "Mandeeeeeeee!"

| Jim Bailey surveyed it all with satisfaction. He'd spent his entire teaching career at Victory High, starting out as a Phys Ed teacher and football coach, finally becoming the school's principal. Tonight was a big deal for him. So far it was going well. The years of planning were paying off.

In recent months, he'd hounded the city's radio stations and newspaper for media coverage. If he could get the school's alumni out this weekend, they'd be more inclined to donate to the sports endowment fund he wanted to establish. And five or ten years from now, they'd come back for another reunion and donate again. Repeatedly, he'd urged his staff to help. Some said he was a little too obsessed with the whole thing. Maybe they were right. But the reunion would be a success: he could feel it in the air.

| Charlotte Andrews drove her mother's sports car toward the city. Jean had made a good choice. The agile little car had a lot of pep. For the first few miles, Charlotte had to remind herself to stay on the right side of the road, but she soon relaxed into the ride. In the last few days, her orphan feeling had vanished. Today, the afternoon sky was clear, an azure umbrella of light and space. Wispy cloud threads wafted above the western horizon.

Charlotte had no intention of actually going to the reunion. Maybe she'd go shopping or take in a movie. At the city limits, she changed her mind, decided that she'd drive by Victory High first, just for a look, so she could describe the scene to her mother, who would want details tomorrow.

She drove around the block twice, looked at the tents, heard the music, smelled the popcorn. Her mother would also want to know what the tent looked like inside, how many people were there, how many familiar faces she'd seen. "You never know who you might run into at something like that," Jean had said as she handed Charlotte the keys.

Her mother's compact car squeezed into a grassy spot between a minivan and a motorcycle. Charlotte paused to watch the end of the volleyball game and recognized her old friend Lisa Martin. Lisa glanced in her direction, but Charlotte couldn't tell whether she recognized her too. Lisa didn't wave, so neither did she.

| Standing at the entrance to the beer tent, Keith Watson asked himself what the hell he was doing. He must've been out of his mind to come. Even his sister Karen had decided against it, saying she'd rather go out to the lake, but Keith knew the real reason: she didn't want to deal with questions about her divorce.

With no intentions of going anywhere on the weekend, Keith had stood on his dock the previous evening, nursing his third rye-and-water, watching an eagle soar and swoop. It snagged a good-sized trout from the lake, but the fish got away, wriggled free, falling back to safety with a splash. The big bird soared off with nothing. Keith had never seen a hooked fish escape from an eagle's talons before.

All through the night, he'd dreamed about fishing, about being in the boat with his niece, Mary Ellen. A smart one, that kid. In the dream, he watched her reel in another fish, but when she turned, she was Kerrie-Lynn. The whole dream was like that: first Mary Ellen, then Kerrie-Lynn, and back to Mary Ellen again. When Keith woke up, instead of his usual shot of vodka, he downed a tomato juice laced with Tabasco sauce. Then he showered and shaved. Soon his boat was skimming over the lake's calm surface.

Now he looked up at the tent's peaked roof and felt small. He glanced around the growing crowd of people and felt smaller. When he saw Coach Bailey walking toward him, he veered off sideways and found himself heading to the bar, where people milled around the bartender, then spilled off into groups at each end, drinks in hand.

Keith's tongue wanted the tart tangy taste of alcohol and its numbing buzz. The smell of hamburgers on a grill drew him toward the food table. He passed a woman holding a mesh sack full of volleyballs. She looked familiar, but he couldn't think of her name.

| With the volleyball game finally over, Lisa Martin packed up the balls and stepped inside the beer tent for a moment, intending to take a quick look around before getting a taxi home. Immediately she knew she'd made a mistake. Jim Bailey rushed up to her. "One of our volunteer cashiers didn't show up. We need help."

Lisa stashed her sack of volleyballs behind the bar and tied on an apron. Back at the tent's entrance, Jim was already chatting with more alumni. He waved at Lisa and gave a cheery thumbs-up. She returned the gesture and started selling hamburgers.

The next time Lisa looked over at the tent entrance, she saw Will talking to Jim. *What was he doing here?* He was holding a girl's hand—the one from the bakery. Will waved at his mother, and Lisa watched as Jim recruited Will to help sell souvenirs at the beanie table.

A few minutes later, Jim came over to thank Lisa for helping out. He pointed over to Will. "Great kid you've got there. I put him to work." Lisa nodded. "And Laura, too. She was a student here a few years ago. Lost her mother in her senior year. Threw her for a loop. It's so good to see her doing better now."

Lisa watched Will and Laura work together, and forgot about the customer she was supposed to be serving.

"Hey. I gave you a twenty and you only gave me four bucks back."

Startled, Lisa handed over a ten, unable to remember whether he'd really given her a twenty or not.

A tall woman with a friendly face stood near the bar. Lisa had seen her watching the volleyball game, but hadn't recognized her until this moment. Charlotte Andrews. Lisa dropped the hamburger she was serving. She fumbled to catch both pieces of the bun before they hit the ground, but missed the meat patty. "Damn!" she said, and handed the guy a whole new burger. She glanced back at the beanie table again. Will and Laura were gone. Charlotte had also disappeared from the bar area.

| More people streamed in, and the beer tent soon bulged at its canvas seams. Victory High alumni jostled their way through the throng, scanning faces as they went. Even unfamiliar faces somehow looked familiar. Jim Bailey wended his way through mobs of former students, greeting them all, shaking hands so often that his fingers began to ache. He took a break, stepped outside to check the sky. It was darkening, the first stars of the night beginning to appear. A breeze rippled through the Victory High banner. The weather was holding. Maybe they'd get those surprise fireworks set off tonight after all.

| Keith was back at the entrance to the big tent. The air had cooled a little, and the tent's flaps fluttered in a small gust of wind. He looked over at the bar again, still wanting and not wanting a drink. Karen had made the right choice. Coming to the reunion had been a mistake. He headed for the exit.

On his way out, Keith walked by the smaller tent. It was less crowded than the beer tent, so he wandered in. The first thing he saw was a display board holding pictures of every graduating class since the school opened twenty-five years ago. Then came a collection of candid photographs certain to embarrass everyone in them. After that, a series of poster-sized prints:

Leo Zawatski's award-winning photo essay from their senior year. Keith examined each photograph closely. The picture that held Keith's attention the longest was the close-up of Roger Andrews. Keith wanted to reach out and touch that jaw, run his hand down the muscles of that neck and shoulder. He also wanted to punch the guy in the face.

| When the crowd started flowing into the beer tent, Leo went outside. He took shots of the whole scene—the kiosks and tents, the banners and balloons. He noticed three women sitting in the grandstand beside the football field. Training his long lens on them, he snapped several shots before he recognized them: the girls who used to ride his Saturday morning bus.

In the small tent, Leo stood in front of his old photos, feeling both pleased and taken aback. Pleased to have these pictures on display again. Pleased to be recognized by his old school. Taken aback because he hadn't looked at these photographs in years, and was surprised at how good they were. He moved through the exhibit, examining each image, lingering over the one of Roger and Coach Bailey, seeing how the coach's arm fell around his quarterback's shoulders, how their faces could hardly contain their victory grins. From there, he moved on to the prom night shots, his old classmates dancing in their tight-fitting suits, homemade satin gowns, and high-heeled shoes. His favourite shot was the one of crushed corsages and bouton-nieres lying on the dance floor.

Two images from the bush party took Leo by surprise. He'd forgotten about them. He moved in close. Illuminated by the bonfire, their faces seemed suspended in space: Amy, Val, Maggie, Kerrie-Lynn, and Keith.

| Leo's photos became a magnet for everyone at the reunion. Word spread about the pictures, and the small tent filled up. Former classmates greeted Leo as a long-lost friend. Leo shook each hand offered and resisted the temptation to say, "So, now you know me?"

Amy couldn't believe the man with the camera and the soft leather jacket was the same guy who used to follow them downtown every Saturday morning. She walked over and held out her hand to him.

"You probably don't remember me. I'm Amy Crawford. Your pictures are magnificent."

| Jim positioned himself at the entrance to the small tent. He wanted to watch the reactions, wanted everyone to look at Roger's picture. Perhaps, most of all, he wanted to look at Roger's picture himself.

Jim knew that he should have known. For almost twenty years, he'd told himself that he should have seen the signs. Back then he'd been a coach for only a few years, and the kid had seemed invincible. Now Jim's desk drawer held a file folder full of articles about football and head injuries. Now he knew what the consequences of untreated concussions were, especially for high-school students. Now he had far more experience dealing with parents who lived vicariously through their children.

But back then, Jim had wanted to prove himself as a coach, wanted both the kids and their parents to like him. So he'd listened to Stan Andrews' constant stream of advice. Even when he knew he should have rested Roger after those crushing hits in the semi-finals, even when he knew he should have made the kid sit out that final game. Stan had insisted that

Roger play: "The boy is tougher than nails. His skull's made of concrete. You can't make him ride the bench."

Yes, Jim knew he should never have listened to Stan. When Roger took more brutal hits in that last game, he should have insisted on a doctor. But they won the game, and euphoria took over. Over the winter, Jim saw Roger playing pickup hockey to stay in shape. When the snow melted that spring, Jim saw Stan and Roger on the football field, starting the spring training routine before winter's chill had left the air. The week before prom night, he came across Roger at his locker, his forehead resting against the door, his hand rubbing the back of his neck. *I'm fine, Coach. Just lots of studying right now.*

Jim also knew he should have protested when Roger's name and pictures disappeared from the school hallways. He was ashamed that he'd retreated into silence, just like everyone else. But that was then and this was now: *This one's for you, kid. You're back.*

| Charlotte moved through the crowd as if on autopilot, unable to turn back. When she arrived in the photo tent, those gathered around the large photo of Roger grew quiet. Many recognized her as Roger's sister. No one had mentioned his name yet, but his portrait made it seem as if he were in the tent with them. A semi-circle formed around Charlotte as she stood looking up at her brother's face.

| Lisa moved into the small tent looking for Will. She felt her knees wobble when she saw the first photo. Part of her wanted to move forward to see the rest, and the other part wanted to flee. The part that controlled her legs took over and moved her

through the display. Yet she froze when she got to the huge photo of Roger, unable to turn away. When she finally pulled her eyes from it, she saw Will and Laura headed directly toward her.

Lisa pushed forward to intercept them, but couldn't get through the crowd. The next thing she knew, Will was beside her.

With Laura on his left and Lisa on his right, Will looked up at the large photograph of the football player. Behind him, the crowd closed in. Then they heard a voice. "Hey, you look just like him."

And then another. And another.

"Yes, he does."

"Wow. What's the word...doppel-something?"

"Doppelganger. No kidding. They're like clones of each other."

And then no one said anything.

Lisa made herself stand still. She knew the moment had come. *Not here. Not now. Not like this.* But it was. Here and now. Like this.

"Who is he?" said Will.

Lisa searched for her voice.

"Mom. Who is he?"

Lisa still said nothing, because she could not take her eyes from Roger's image. It had been so many years since she'd looked at that face, seen those eyes, heard that voice. *Don't forget to breathe.* She turned to her son. "His name was Roger."

"And is there a reason that I look so much like this Roger guy?"

"Yes," said Lisa.

By this time, Charlotte Andrews was standing right beside Lisa, with Keith Watson on her other side. Beside him was Leo, still studying the photos of the bush party.

Amy, Maggie, and Val clustered behind Will and Lisa. All had their eyes on Roger's picture, except for Amy, who was watching Leo. In the background, the DJ was playing "Bohemian Rhapsody," with Freddie Mercury's voice rising audible above the fray: "Mama..."

"I've been trying to figure out everyone in this shot." Leo pointed at the bonfire photo. "Keith, I think that's you in the background. What's that in your hand?"

Maggie leaned in and studied the image. "It looks like a roll of duct tape."

Keith's voice was flat. "I didn't know. I didn't know what he wanted that damn tape for. He said he needed to fix something in his van. I had a roll in my pack."

Leo thought he heard moaning. Did it come from someone beside him? Or maybe it was the wind?

Charlotte didn't know what to say or do. Her brother's image was so clear, he seemed alive. And beside her was this young apparition, Roger's double. Next to him, Lisa's face was ashen. And now this skinny guy with the yellow skin said he gave her brother the duct tape Roger had used on his van that night.

Charlotte turned. The crowd divided in two, making a path for her to leave. She tried not to run.

| Lisa was shaking when Jim finally reached her. He put his arm around her shoulders, and she sagged against him. Jim looked from Will to Roger's picture, and back to Will, seeing something else he should have known.

Will turned to his mother. "How did he die?"

Jim answered for Lisa. "Carbon monoxide poisoning. After the prom."

Will looked back at his father's picture. "I don't understand. Why would he do that? Because of me?"

Lisa shook her head. "Because of me."

| "Look at how beautiful Kerrie-Lynn was," said Maggie, still at the bonfire photo.

Maggie would have crawled inside that picture if she could have. She touched her friend's face with her index finger.

"What happened to you?" she asked again.

Keith heard Maggie's words, and moved closer. He didn't need to look at his twin sister's picture. He saw her in his mind every day. Looking around the tent filled with his former classmates, he hesitated. *Should I tell the whole story? About Roger and Kerrie-Lynn? About the abortion two weeks after grad night?* He caught a glimpse of Will. The kid who had just found his father was still gazing up at Roger's larger-than-life image.

"Kerrie-Lynn was bipolar," Keith said. "Six months after she left for California, I went to see her. She was off her meds. Asked me to get her some sleeping pills. I didn't know she'd been hoarding pills. I got her ten more that night. Doctor of death, that's me."

| The crowd in the small tent didn't hear the silence that fell over them because a roar came from outside. No one had noticed how much the wind had picked up over the last hour, that the big beer tent was now almost deserted because the air had grown cold, that the parking lot was half-empty, that people were taking shelter in the school. Then the wind tore the photo tent open.

A great whoosh filled the space and the tent lifted. Higher and higher until it was airborne—a swirling white kite set free, photographs and beanie hats rising up with it, its whiteness illuminated against the sky by the lights around the skating rink.

Everyone standing where the photo tent had been seconds earlier ran for the school. Everyone except for Leo and Amy. Leo fell to one knee and aimed his camera upwards, at the white canvas spinning sideways and upwards and sideways again.

Amy watched Leo's every move. She watched him drop to the ground, lie on his back, camera still aimed at the sky. She watched him get back up and turn his lens on her. She wondered why she'd never noticed him back in school. Only when the rain came did they run for cover.

The storm had taken all evening to brew, but after it hit, it dissipated in minutes. People emerged to a shattered venue. The beer tent was still standing, but askew. The food kiosks were upended, beer cans were scattered across the grounds among soaked beanies, pompoms, and torn canvas. Most of the photos were ruined, but the large image of Roger had survived. The alumni of Victory High took it with them when they moved their reunion to the nearest hotel bar. Roger was at the centre of the party for the rest of the night.

| The next morning, Will and Laura worked in Lisa's back yard cleaning up wind-blown branches. Lisa watched Will, trying to gauge what was happening in his head. Earlier, she'd told him she would answer any question he needed to ask. He said he didn't have any questions at the moment, but that he'd let her know when he did. He told her not to worry. But he didn't hug her.

Lisa felt the distance between them as she worked in one corner of the yard, Will and Laura in another.

When Jim Bailey walked through the gate, Lisa's pulse quickened.

"Am I fired?"

"What? No. Of course not. I just wanted to make sure you're okay."

"We're fine," said Lisa, glancing over at Will. "Well, maybe not totally fine, but we will be."

"I hope you don't mind, but I brought a friend."

Charlotte appeared from around the corner. "I'm sorry I left so fast last night. It was a bit of a shock."

"I understand," said Lisa, trying to keep her own voice steady. She beckoned for Will to join them. He crossed the yard in seconds.

"Will, I want you to meet Charlotte. An old friend of mine from my university days." Lisa studied her son's face before continuing. "She's also your aunt."

Charlotte held out her hand. "I'm pleased to meet you, Will." Will took her hand in his.

Charlotte covered their two hands with her other one. "I feel like I'm looking at my brother," she said. "It's uncanny. This will take some getting used to. For both of us, I'm sure."

Will nodded. Jim shuffled his feet.

Lisa's skin felt itchy all over. She scratched at her arms. "Coffee, anyone?"

Charlotte pointed toward the street. "I know this might be too quick, but I'm heading back to Australia soon. Before I go, there's someone out front who wants to meet you, Will."

Charlotte led the way, followed by Lisa and Will, with Laura and Jim trailing behind. The group walked single file, stepping over downed branches along the narrow path beside Lisa's house. A light breeze had replaced last night's whirling wind. The sky was clear, the morning air calm, scented with lilac from a row of bushes blooming mauve and white.

The red sports car was parked on the street. Sitting in the passenger seat, an old photo album resting on her lap, Jean Andrews waited to meet her grandson.

Acknowledgments

This book has been a long time in the making. For their invaluable help during its extended gestation, I will be forever grateful to these wonderful people.

To everyone at University of Alberta Press: you are a great team, a joy to work with. A special shout-out goes to Peter Midgley for his consistent support every step of the way.

To my editor, the marvellous Helen Moffett: I am so lucky—I've now worked with Helen on two books. As an editor, she is a writer's dream: demanding, astute, funny, prodding, generous, and wise.

To Kimmy Beach: for superb project guidance, working wine o'clock Skype sessions, and always-there friendship. This book would still be an abandoned pile of papers in a bottom drawer if some external force hadn't prompted me to pull it out and ask Kimmy to read it.

To Katherine Koller: for bringing her keen sense of narrative and sharp eyes to my words.

To the late Holley Rubinsky, for the hours on her Kaslo veranda, along with Dianne Linden and Linda Crosfield, my colleagues at Holley's "Bear-Banger" Writing Retreat in 2012.

To Zsuzsi Gartner, a whirlwind whiz when it comes to storytelling, and the Literary Arts Program at the Banff Centre, specifically Zsuzsi's "Writing with Style" Short Fiction group, April 2011.

And last but always first, to my husband George and my family: for their life-saving buoyancy and constant love.